SHELLHORN LEGACY

Cover Design by Sabertooth Book Services

First edition 2023

Paperback ISBN: 9798395145802

SHELLHORN LEGACY

Book I

By Brian Kerr

Contents

Chapter 1

Garrett Shellhorn

David Shellhorn remembered as a toddler Great Grandfather Garrett; the Dutchman born in the Netherlands. Bouncing him on his knee or down kneeling on all fours entertaining him with play and travel adventure stories. As a 15-year youth, Garrett travelled on foot working and acquiring skills across Western Europe. Later he sailed on a tall, masted ship across to Morocco, Africa. Garrett told his stories. "I had a lust for the riches of Africa". "Then I was not yet a rich man. I was ambitious and had a powerful work ethic. In the year 1902 as a 20-year-old man I had considered working in the slave business. Young men could find entry work on the auction block selling slaves. There was still plenty of money to be made selling enslaved men. African nations have always taken slaves as profits of war. Slaves are a commodity traded as wealth and can be sold as war treasures. The world economies provide a robust auction market to sell African slaves to. Perhaps as many as 10,000,000 Abel bodied men, women and children were removed from the continent of Africa" Slavery is a nasty business. I wanted nothing to do with it."

"Gold is always worth seeking if you can find it." Storied Great Grandpa Shellhorn. "If you are willing to work hard and take great risks. A man can find others to share the burden and employ the skill to find precious gold. The best way to improve your chances of striking it rich is to become an industrious gold miner and employer of men. For more than a decade I panned then mined for riches. Working alone panning rivers, then employing others to expand the productive efforts in mines."

"I eventually travelled from the north of Morocco to the far end of the Continent reaching the Horn of South Africa. I travelled by ship, by camel and even by mule. Seldom by rail. Africa was a wild continent then. Always fighting Continental war. Too hostile to connect individual countries by rail. Travel was slow and dangerous. I lived with daily fear. The fear of being robbed or worse being killed for my possessions." Even having a gun to protect me gave me little solace sitting vulnerable on a camel or an ass. Of course, I travelled with armed merchants. Africa was a land of desperate hungry men. Black, Brown, and white."

"I had made money and I had lost money mining gold. I was slowly improving my wealth. I became an expert in the mining business. I was looking for gold in the Horn of Africa. I competed with miners from every corner of the globe who had converged there to strike it rich. It was the biggest gold rush ever witnessed on earth. Many miners got rich. Most did not. I had a crew of good men working for me, a few white, and many black men. Regardless of race, I offered an ounce of gold to any man that found a rich deposit of minerals. A miner by the name of Muhamed came to find me to claim his ounce of gold. I immediately found an African language to English interpreter. The three of us proceeded down into the mine. When I illuminated the excavated rock expecting to find gold. To my astonishment, a magnificent precious diamond shone back at me. At that moment, the brilliance of

an 83./5 carats diamond shone back at me. I
named the diamond the Star of Africa that would
later prove to be a perfect cut white diamond of
47.69 karats."

"It made me a wealthy man. I understood at that
very moment I would never sell the White Star of
Africa. I would store it in a Swiss Vault protecting
my wealthy status for my entire life. I have the rest
of my life to add to my riches. The year was 1907."

"I was 25 when the White Star of Africa diamond
was found. I had 119 men employed in the South
African mine, mostly Black miners. They worked
damn hard. A dollar a day wages could keep them
from starving. They dug straight down deep into the
earth with a pick and shovel. They sifted through
the dirt discovering many diamonds. I will tell you
the Negros were the best damn workers. They had
an unbelievable hunger for survival money. Many
black Africans without work starved to death."

"Some people mistakenly thought working the
mines was the most dangerous job."

"The man who had the most dangerous job ever in
my employ was the security officer and French
man Altair. I put Altair in charge of transporting the
exclusive White Star of Africa diamond to safety.
Danger strikes quickly in the mines. Word can

travel fast when a mine strikes a rare diamond. Muhamed was a lucky Nigerian miner who did retire with his gold coin reward. It wasn't him that spoiled the secret discovery of the Star of Africa diamond. He was safe at home."

"Some miners believe the walls of the mine are the revelation of hidden treasures. Of course, that is nonsense. By the time Altair transported the diamond to the light of day a sinister group of desperados was ready to take the claim. Word has gotten out; a fantastical diamond is being secreted to safety. Fifty or more men armed with pickaxe shovels and some with forbidden machetes lunged for Altair and his men to take the Star of Africa diamond. Altair brandishing a multi round pistol flanked by two loyal African long riflemen opened fire on the mob. Altair retreated to secure the prized diamond. The mele was not broken up until a cliff top cannon was brought into position and fired. Fortunately, The Diamond" and Altair were safeguarded. It was a sorrowful loss that the two forward standing African long riflemen were hacked to pieces by machetes. The families of the deceased were given compensation. I am a fair man. Other white mine owners did not want to start giving any extra compensation to black workers whom they considered expendable."

"When I retired much later in 1969 my mines employed over a thousand workers. The geologists and security people were mainly white. During the early years of mining, we had the black African miners work nearly naked with leather loincloths. Humiliating but practical. No hidden diamonds in clothing, simple but effective. They were paid enough to show up for work and bring their talents. It was the African negro workers that made the big money for all the mines. I still don't Know why the Negros worked so hard for so little money."

"In 1922 we mined enough diamonds to ship direct to Europe on a regular basis. I decided to start up a small shipping company to safeguard the shipment of gold and diamonds from South Africa to England, France, and Italy. To secure safe passage of our gold minted to coin and bars and diamonds to be cut into precious gems. The uncut diamonds, gold dust and nuggets were safeguarded aboard ships with fast modern steam engines and heavy armament to safeguard our journey to European Ports. The business was small to begin with. We secured shipping contracts to bring back fine wines, brandies, and gin. As well as machinery equipment for the mines. Transactions were secured with government issued gold and silver bars. A tidy profit was made. I hired honest, reliable men to guard our treasures. Soon demand from other mining and ivory exports wanted secure passage shipped to the continent. I formed the African Shellhorn Trading Company ASTC. to attract investors 1925 was a very good year". "I was able to employ my son Abel Shellhorn, your grandfather. He set sail in 1925 from England to Johannesburg, my son, Able, was the man that made the greatest family fortune. Abel transformed the North African Shipping Company into an international enterprise handling valuable commodities by air and by sea around the world. I didn't have time or money to attend college. Abel made valuable social connections from his many affluent investors. I am an old-fashioned adventurer. Abel graduated from the prestigious English Cambridge University. I was always proud to have a Cambridge graduate son. I was pleased with the financial investments he made for the family business. I must admit it bothered me that my son made four times the money I did with one quarter of the physical work. I Made sure that my son Abel knew what physical work is. The first thing I did when Abel arrived in Johannesburg was to put him to work in the mine with the Negro miners. It did him good, there is no harm in hard work, son. Abel had the markings of a great businessman. He has good family pedigree and inherits the good intelligence of a Shellhorn man.

He was willing to work hard while employing ruthless vigour."

"When it came time for Abel to choose a college. There was only one choice for him. The University of Cambridge. The University was world renowned. It has a celebrated history. So, when Abel Shellhorn was concerned that he might not be accepted as a student to Cambridge he wrote to me in Africa asking for my assistance. Upon reading of my son's request, I wrote a business letter to the President Tomlin of the University of Cambridge."

August 20, 1921

DEAR MR. PRESIDENT TOMLIN:

I AM INCREDIBLY PLEASED MY SON ABEL SHELLHORN HAS WORKED DILIGENTLY TO SERVE AS A STUDENT AT ENGLAND'S OLDEST AND FINEST UNIVERSITY. I AM CERTAIN THAT ONCE HE HAS GAINED ADMISSION TO ATTEND CLASSES AT THE UNIVERSITY OF CAMBRIDGE THAT HE WILL SHOW MERIT AND BE A COMPLEMENT TO STUDENTS AND STAFF.

I AM ENCLOSING A CHECK AS A DONATION OF $3000. I HAVE WORKED HARD MINING FOR GOLD AND DIAMONDS IN THE GREAT CONTINENT OF AFRICA. I AM A MAN OF MY WORD. YOU CAN EXPECT ANOTHER $3000. CHECK AT THE START OF MY BOY'S SECOND YEAR OF UNIVERSITY CLASSES.

SINCERELY, GARRETT SHELLHORN

Abel was the first of my family to graduate from college. During four years at the University of Cambridge Abel was a capable learner taking coursework in History, Maths and International Commerce. The city of Cambridge dated back 3500 years to Roman times. The first University of Cambridge was founded in 1209. Abel was Abel to learn of the rise and fall, triumphs, and defeats at Europe's oldest University. He pursued bicycling and the sport of rowing in an idealised environment of pride and privilege. Though Abel did not long remain in the company of the Cambridge's Aristocracy. He did fraternise with many ambitious young men. Most importantly Abel more than paid back the family investment. That his father Garrett Shellhorn made for his son to attend Cambridge University.

Garrett Shellhorn indeed expected payback from his Cambridge tuition that he paid for his son's attendance at the University of Cambridge. He expected payback in the form of a business partnership uniting the two Shellhorn men in a commercial adventure. To be successful in this adventure he would need to earn the boys trust. Abel is now 15 years of age, nearly a man. He had followed the boy's progress and responded with him. He had written many letters offering fatherly council. Both he and his mother were always kept financially secure in London. Yet Garrett worried he needed personal contact with Abel. Abel had never had the opportunity to bond in person with his father. Garrett would have to think of a plan for the family to unite and enjoy some family bonding time. Garrett is confident that given the chance he can capture the hearts of both his wife and son. Tonight, after he turned in for the evening, he would search in his sleep to find a solution. With luck in the morning Garrett would awaken with a plan.

Garrett is refreshed in the morning with a good night's sleep Garrett has a splendid idea. They could all go on a family European cruise. He will send an invitational telegram to his wife, Laura. He will not risk rejection. He will simply inform them when and where they are going. Yes, father knows best!

The telegram read.

DEAREST LAURA. I HAVE MADE ARRANGEMENTS FOR OUR FAMILY TO GO ON A EUROPEAN FAMILY CRUISE. I AM NO LONGER A YOUNG MAN. I NEED FAMILY TIME. I WILL WRITE WITH THE DETAILS.

GARRETT

Dearest Laura,

Abel is a 15 year old man. At the age of 15, I walked out of the Netherlands and began a successful career as an African miner. It is high time I begin to groom my son to inherit my family business. A cruise will be the perfect opportunity for him and I to get acquainted in person for the first time. In a few short years the lad will attend his University studies. As you know I never had the time and money to attend collegiate studies. I look forward to carrying the financial burden while Abel pursues his studies. The day will come when Abel will be expected to contribute to the family business and apply his education and worldly connections to the Shellhorn Shipping business.

Sincerely, Garrett

Abel knew for certain that the friendly jovial man that accompanied him and his mother, on a European cruise at the age of 15, would be a much different man to work for. No fun could be had from the hard mining work Garret envisioned for his son.

The 23-year-old Abel could have no idea what lay ahead of him. After many weeks at sea Abel Shelhorn disembarked from his 1800-mile journey. He had been too sick and lacking acceptable food to eat much of anything. Gaunt and sickly he went to meet his father.

First, he prayed for redemption. Sanitary food and shelter. His prayers went unanswered.

The first thing Garrett said to his son was. "Christ son you look like hell. I am proud of you for coming down here to work with your dad. We will make one hell of a team. First let's get you cleaned up and then have something to eat. We don't have hot water to shower in. Abel loved his hot baths and had never showered in cold water before. The cold-water showers would later prove to be invigorating." Garret said. "You can tell me all about your travels while we eat dinner, son. Tomorrow I will start teaching you the business of mining."

Garrett updated Abel concerning the recent historical events that had impacted the family mining business. "We have found that we are right in the middle of a three-sided war being fought by African, Dutch and English. Our goal is to survive the war and eventually prosper. The African Black people who are the original inhabitants and have by far the greatest number of people living on the continent find themselves at a great disadvantage. They are the least successful in obtaining modern armaments. The Dutch from Holland who were first to colonise and prosper in the South African mines are evidently second to England in Military might. An alliance was made in 1899 allying the African tribal Kaffirs and Zulus with the Dutch Boers against the British military backed forces. Unfortunately, In 1902 the British forces were victorious, Britain took control of South Africa. The British celebrated their win by levying a mining tax to pay for the debts of war."

The Dutch East India Company in 1652 established a city as a halfway point for trade from East to West in Johannesburg, South Africa. The Dutch and French colonised the new city . They intermarried and profited from shipping commerce and the slave trade The British came to lay siege in 1849.They freed the slaves creating racial tensions that are still in dispute today. Africa is the continent that has the most Black inhabitants. When the British attempted to stop the profitable trade of slaves they failed to share income and resources in an equitable manner. Freeing slaves earned the British goodwill with the African Negro that they used to leverage against the French and Dutch interest. British profits grew from colonial taxation all the while profiting from low Black wages.

During the Boer war of 1899 the British imposed martial law mandating that all productive mines remain open. The British financed the cost of the war by taxing the mines. Any mine that stopped production was taken possession by the English and pressed back into business. Dutch mines were allowed to remain Dutch Colonial owned so long as the British Imperial taxes were paid. Of course, having an English mother living in London was of little economic benefit to the Dutch man Garrett Shellhorn. Garret kept ownership of his mines but suffered from heavy British taxation. Garrett loved his English son and wife. He maintained a lifetime hatred of the insufferable Brits.

Abel however first and foremost considered himself to be of good British accent. Abel was grateful that His father didn't attack his own maternal English lineage. Abel remembered his mother's storied intolerance to living in Johannesburg, Africa. When his father Garrett Shellhorn first courted then married his mother, Laura Stanley. They lived in Johannesburg, South Africa. She was 18 years old when they met. She had travelled to Africa to visit an aunt living there. Laura had met Garrett at a formal dance social. Garret, 19 years older than her. He had quite literally swept her off her feet. He told marvellous stories of travel and riches. She had spent a scandalous night with the confident bachelor. She returned home to her aunt's home being none the wisers. 8 weeks after Laura returned to London, she discovered she was pregnant. Laura's parents convinced her honour required her to return to Africa to sort things out with the unborn baby's father.

A hasty marriage was arranged. Abel Shellhorn was conceived and born in South Africa. After a several month trial marriage, both Garrett and Laura conceded that they were incompatible. Laura fled back to London Upon their return, baby Abel was baptised at the Church of England. His African birth was never spoken of again. Abel had taken his mother's Stanley name in London . He would be recorded as a Stanley descendant amongst 500 years' baptismal records at the Anglican Church of England on the official Stanley Registry.

Able's mining endeavours with his father in South Africa required resumption of Garret's "Shellhorn" family name at his father's insistence. In the year 1939 a man could easily change his name without legal paperwork. It would have been an unacceptable embarrassment to reside with a mother or father and have a different family name. Garrett continued financial responsibility for his son and wife. He and Laura maintained a civil relationship two continents apart. Family bonds were maintained by written correspondence.

Abel would try his best to win the respect of his Dutch father. Today would not be an easy day. Abel descended into the mines surrounded by rugged Black miners. They had never seen such soft tender hands wrapped around a miner's pickaxe. Abel left the mine at the end of the day his hands red of clay and blood caked dry. He was still gaunt and sickly from his arduous voyage to Africa. In one day's time he was not so different from the neglected Black miners he worked with. With absolute certainty he hated his father's despotism. He would become like his English mother. Proper and reserved Abel the Englishman. Now he hates his father. His mother's family no longer acknowledged Africa as Able's place of birth. The Abel Stanley name ends when Garret and son merge business ventures. Abel inherits his mother's civility and refinement. It is the Dutch Shellhorn name that Abel will pass onto his descendants.

While working in the mine his father would remain an estranged fierce father that offered comfort with food and lodging. As Abel toiled in the diamond mine They both used silence as a weapon. After one year of hard labour in the mines Abel was released from servitude to pursue his destiny in the family shipping business. Little did Abel realise, A Second World War and many war U boat torpedo disasters lay ahead for the Shellhorn Shipping Company. Able's education at Cambridge sharpened his intellectual skills. Working in the mine toughened his resolve. He is ready to prosper the family wealth.

Garrett hoped someday Abel could appreciate that he wanted what was best for his son. He also hoped Abel could someday repay him for all those years of financial support that he had given the boy in school and home in England. Garrett thought maybe somehow, they could patch their relationship as father and son. Secretly Garett knew that for most of Able's life he was never there. It was Laura who raised Able. She has done a good job. Father and son hopefully have gainful years ahead of them. There should be plenty of time to make things better.

Abel left the mine with the conviction to never ever return to the mines. For one year he had entered the diamond mine in the early morning darkness. Only to depart into the darkness of the night. Going to lodge with the Dutchman, his father. Slowly a modem of strength crept in. The filth of the African soils never completely washed off in the cold showers that he learned to love, a much gentler experienced pain than working in the mines.

Unlike the many black and few White and Asian miners. Abel had a home with running potable water and flavorful prepared food. Food that tasted good, almost too good. Those poor bastards he worked with had it much worse. They knew it. Abel knew it too. Yet they were kind to him, even respectful. Was this what the old man was trying to teach him? Abel would never know the answer to these questions. He and his father kept their distance, seldom speaking. The two men each had dark thoughts that they both intended not to share. Time can heal some of these wounds. Garret and Abel eventually discovered a kind of respect and admiration in the later productive shipping years.

For a creature of darkness, it is not easy to enter the light. The first week out of the mines Abel drank heavily. For seven straight days he got drunk and stayed drunk. The alcohol helped him to survive the nightmares. The old man 's home is spartan, however the liquor cabinet and wine cellar are well provisioned. Abel is all too familiar with the inventory.

Lying in bed at night, Abel would dream he was trapped inside a falling mine. In his dream he would struggle against falling rock and timber. Initially having success then failing to recover from additional cave-ins. They ended when he awakened in a cold sweat fearing death. Abel had another recurring dream. He dreamt he was going blind. Darkness would seep in like a heavy fog. As the darkness progressed less and less was illuminated until Abel remained in suffocating darkness. Blind. African miners of that era had some moments of complete and utter darkness, as lights were prone to failure. How could Abel or you or I know what fear went on in the minds of miners of old?

"I am a Cambridge man. Dammit" Abel thought. "I have got to pull myself away from this life." A cleansed and sober Abel approached his father, Garret, to request financial assistance and a new opportunity . "Father, I am ready to take responsibility for running our shipping business. I will require money to return to Europe. I believe I can secure financial investors in London. Capital Investments that will allow our shipping business to expand far beyond Western Europe and Africa. I intend to be self-sufficient. I plan to draw my wages from the shipping businesses profits." Garret responded. "Son, I know I put you through hell working in the mines. It can be nasty work. Some day you may thank me for it. I needed for you to understand and appreciate where the shipping business money came from. I wanted you to appreciate what hard work is. I am certain that is something they don't teach to your Cambridge privileged classmates. Then the old Dutchman said something that stuck with his son. "Able You got my Dutch blood running through you. "You are tougher than the English. You survived in the mines where weaker men would have failed." Abel thought his father would have preferred him dead rather than have a weak son, Garrett might admit this to be true. Garrett also knew that South Africa had many more Dutchmen braving the dangers of the mine than Englishmen. Abel soon left South Africa behind realising being a Dutch and English blend could be something to be proud of. Abel truly had become a better man.

Garrett demonstrated to his son, Abel for the first time in Africa how trusting and generous he could be. He gave full control of operations of the African Shellhorn Trading company, ASTC. to his son, Able. That included full access to revenues and expenses Garrett Shellhorn remained the sole proprietor. Abel was made the chief executive of the shipping business. Abel was also given first class travel expenses to return to Europe. When Abel disembarked for London, his mood was buoyant, and he felt renewed. He had his own Shipping company and the entire world of opportunities lay ahead of him.

Source Material

Able Shellhorn Journal: 1918 to 1970

Archived to family history

Submitted June 17, 1973

Chapter 2

Family Cruise

It was a complete surprise Abel was to meet his father for the first time at age 15. His mother Laura announced. "Able your father Garrett will soon be coming home to England." Garrett Shellhorn had travelled to Africa as a young man, perhaps to never return to Europe." Now he has booked a European cruise for himself, his wife and son. They will depart London on the 15th of March 1913. Laura Shellhorn read the telegraph repeatedly half in disbelief before she shared the news with her 15 year old son, Able. She knew the day would come when she would have to share her son with his father since she had fled home to London. Abel was baptised and raised in the long 500 year line of English Stanleys. In a few short years he hopefully would attend Cambridge University. Garret had reluctantly agreed to the terms of separation so long ago. She would raise their son to be a proper Englishman. Abel would take her English maiden name, Stanley. Technically Abel will have dual ancestry, English and Dutch. Laura had agreed that Abel would be provided whatever business opportunity his father could provide after his university graduate studies. Laura dreaded the day her husband would take custody of Abel and her son would resume the family name of Shellhorn.

Laura did not know what to think of this cruise intervention. She also knew Garrett could be a most forceful man. She would wait for his arrival. She would protect her son's English heritage, then make the best of things.

Garrett Shellhorn had excellent timing to squeeze in a family adventure before the ravages of WWI and the Spanish flu onset. Further communication revealed the family would be. Traveling comfortably in second class. Garrett also promised they would have access to first class amenities as a guest to an affluent Dutch cousin, Fenn Shellhorn who was sure to invite them as a welcomed social guest to first class amenities. Garrett sent money to them for a seagoing travel chest and to purchase appropriate evening wear.

Abel at the age of 15 believed he was privileged to be a young man with a kind mother and a father that could provide generously for the two of them. Abel was acquainted with other boys who were raised only by their mothers. These boys believed they had a little more leeway without a strict male disciplinarian. Now for the first time in his life he would have the acquaintance of his father. Garrett too had his concerns. Could he enter his young adult son's life and form a father and son bond? Garrett entertained the idea that a trifle of romance could be enjoyed with his absent wife Laura. He would not hold his breath.

If Garrett was going to enjoy a European cruise with his family the first thing he would need to do was travel to London. Simplicity would be in order. No luxury cruise ship for his trip. Garret found passage on an Ocean Liner transit from Johannesburg to London. Launched the 29th of June, 1889 and updated in 1903 as the English White Star Line RMS Majestic. Built solid for the Royal Navy she could be accessed in time of war. She could travel an impressive 20 knotts. Later scrapped in May 1914.

Garrett Shelhorn travelled to England via deck side third class on the Majestic. He was satisfied with the furnishings of a deck rug and chair. The best part of the cruise was the ample supply of fresh sea breeze. He took with him two litres of quinine gin and a supply of a dozen limes. Garret could be a progressive man. The quinine drove away the tropical malaria and the limes were useful in countering scurvy. Mr. Shellhorn was a man ahead

of his times. Upon arriving in London Garrett
claimed the cruise was the best cruise in his life.
The man would go on to enjoy many cruises. He
later would claim the simplicity of the majestic
cruise was his all-time favorite voyage.

Abel and his mother Laura entered the London
Selfridges Department Store one week before their
cruise departure. They both looked forward to
purchasing some fun and practical clothing for the
cruise. They picked a time and a place to meet
inside the store to pay for their purchases. 15-year-
old Abel was feeling mature and grown up as he
headed off to the Menswear Department. He was
looking for something fun yet practical. After a
lengthy search he happened on what he wanted to
buy. Selfridge buyers had brought in new casual
fashion from the American Levi Straus company.
Abel found a pair of 501 jeans and a matching
Denim jacket. Eagerly he gathered up the correct
size then took off to find his mother. While waiting
for her return he hoped his mother would allow the
purchase of these bold fashions. Laura returned to
the rendezvous with a lovely floral Spring dress
and complementary shoes. This was her first
shopping trip for fashion in years. Her face was
flush with excitement. When she first saw Able's
new wardrobe she wasn't quite sure what to think.

Laura took one look at Able's face and gave her dismissive support.

One week later, father and son with wife in tow walked up the entry ramp. Garrett took one look at the coarse Levi fabric that Abel was wearing and ground his teeth in quiet disapproval. Garrett thought if I had been in London to parent my child he would have grown up to dress more respectable . Nothing was ever said. Garrett carried their sea travel trunk aboard. Laura chose to take a large purse with her. It contained travel treats. A one litre bottle of Bombay gin for Garrett. A large bar of Swiss chocolate for Abel and a Dutch box of tea biscuits for her. The large purse would be replenished during the European stops. Treats aboard the ship are expensive, It is best to bring their own favourites.

.8:00 AM the 15 of March 1913. The RMS Olympic pulled away from the dock with all 2,435 full capacity passengers. Sounding the deep sound of the departure horn. The loud sound startled many of the passengers. Garrett and Abel were boyishly entertained. Laura couldn't help but be pleased that a solid father and son bond was beginning. She entertained the idea that if Garrett were to become a London businessman life could be so different. Laura knew such thoughts were impractical. Slowly the many passengers found assistance amongst the 450 crew members to settle in first-, second- and third-class accommodations.

The crew and passengers took part in a very special marine history. The 882 feet long RMS Olympic would leave on its maiden passenger voyage to be registered as the only un- sunk vessel in the White Line Class after the Second World War. The sister ship the RMS Britannia was sunk as a hospital ship during WWI. Germany did replace Britannia as war reparations. On the 15th of March there was much talk of war. The great war had not yet started.

Travelling second class had significant advantages compared to the third class. They have full indoor protection from the sea. The new ship met its first Full Gale force winds immediately after leaving the English Coast. Mountains of waves some reaching 45 feet in height. The Shellhorn family had a bit of double luck. They enjoyed a superior vantage to lessen motion sickness. Their cabin has 6 tables. Had a clear view of the bow of the ship as it rose into the air. The giant waves pushed the bow starboard. The helmsman corrected the port to keep the ship heading on as straight a course as possible. Cresting the wave, the bow would plunge into the trough far below. At the bottom of the wave trough the bow of the ship would dig into the approaching wave sending ocean spray flying back to the bridge. If a passenger can keep their cookies down it is a glorious experience. There are two keys to success. One should maintain a clear view of the wave action to anticipate the rise and fall of the ship. Two; avoid the stench of other seasick passengers. The odiferous air of the ill at sea is all but a guarantee of even the most hardy getting seasick to join the fate of the sour stomach. If a person starts to feel ill a trip outside to fresh air is prudent. Hours later the RMS Olympic rounded the South end of Great Britain. Away from tumultuous wind and tidal currents the ocean waves subsided some. Cousin Fenn Shelhorn popped into the cabin to invite the men for a smoke. Laura decided to investigate the boat deck side.

Laura was invigorated by the Atlantic sea air. She could see many a deck chair lay strewn about. The third-class passengers appeared to be wet and shivering As she walked from the bow aft to stern the condition of the passengers' health seemed to deteriorate. Laura came upon an elderly couple that appeared green around the gills. Laura approached to assist. "May I offer you some help." Please follow me forward so that you can find your sea legs. Slowly the old pair of travellers made their way to the view of the bow. Laura promised they could take the departed seats of her socialising husband and son. They were off enjoying men's talk and a seat in the smoking parlour. Once they settled their tummies and warmed up a bit. Laura was sure they would feel better. She was right, they just needed a little human compassion. The guest's name is Clampetts. They travelled all the way from Louisville, Kentucky, U.S.A. to celebrate their 50th wedding anniversary. Each following day a game of musical chairs played out. The Shellhorn men would go to the smoking parlour with cousin Fenn Shellhorn. The Clampetts would come inside to join Laura for tea and biscuits. Travel without the social is about as useful as a bucket with a hole in it.

While Laura was entertaining the Clampetts, Garrett and Abel accompanied Fenn Shellhorn to the first-class smoking room. As they strolled their way to the men's club Fenn described the incredible portable Turkish bath that he found to be rejuvenating. The new RMS Olympic was outfitted with the same state of the art electric baths as the Titanic, another member of the White line. The bath consisted of a green sheet-metal lid equipped with several ultraviolet lamps utilising metal clamps that could provide the bather complete tanning exposure. Users would open the lid then recline upon a wooden stand. The bath attendant would close the lid and set the timer. Then presto the bather would come out with a perfect tan. Sure enough Fenn sported a perfect tan. Fenn remarked. "What will they think of next?" Before the men approached the smoking parlour. Abel was coached to look the entry guardian in the eye and tell him he was 20 years of age. The smoking lounge is a "Men's Only Club." Abel did as he was told. It must have helped that Garrett palmed a generous tip to the smoke Club's guardian. Just like that Abel was a welcome member every day since Garrett had his son outfitted for smoking before the cruise departure. Abel accompanied him to London's Briar Pipes. To select suitable smoking supplies to be enjoyed aboard the RMS Olympic in the first-class passenger smoking parlour. He coached his son to select a smaller novice pipe that would be easy to keep lit. Abel selected a burl wood bowl, Garrett thought it looked very sporting and mature. With the new pipe in hand Abel tested various flavoured tobaccos. Barret purchased his son a light Virginian tobacco with a hint of cherry flavour. Barret purchased a half dozen Cuban cigars for himself. They were cruise ship ready.

Smoking in the ship's parlour was hazy, lazy and delightful. That is until the conversation turned to war and politics. 16 Months after the ship's maiden voyage German U- Boats would be the top predator in the Atlantic. No ships would find a guaranteed safe passage. The tension leading up to WWI were prevalent in the Spring of 1913. Aboard that very ship were Austrians, Germans Austria- Hungary and Italians The Triple Alliance Vs. Triple Entente, Consisting of French, Russian and Britons. On one hand it was a civil smoke room. On the other hand, it could be a pre- war room. Smoking is meant to be a peaceful experience. Civilising. It was natural to seek the refuge of your own kinsmen. Yet the occasion would arrive when pride and prejudice flared. England fought the one-hundred-year war with neighbouring France; it lasted from 1337 to 1453. Protestant England fought four additional wars for the empire against Catholic France in the eighteenth century. Prior to the start of WWI England was by far the dominant world Naval power and global empire builder. During World War I it chose to be allied with France. England needed any and all allies to thwart the might of the Triple Alliance. Soon soldiers of the English Colonies. America, no longer a colony, threw its support to England, suffering more than a million casualties in four years of fighting in the trenches.

Gaston Rutherford the Frenchman approached Fenn and Garret. Knowing they spoke English Gaston asked in hushed English. "I hope that when the German military advances on Holland you will join France with England and march against

Bismarck's Germany. Garrett put aside his imperial differences. Garrett spoke first. "My wife is English." I will fight for her honour. You won't find me or my friend Fenn fighting for the Germans. Gaston excused his leave and returned shortly with lounge crystal tumblers of fine French brandy. The three comrades basked in the warmth of smoke, brandy and good will. The two Dutchmen would never know that in two years' time lieutenant Rutherford Would die on a failed attempt to lead his men out of the trenches rallied against the dug in German line.

The first Port of call after leaving London is Marseille, France this Port city dates back to 600 BC. Sandy Mediterranean beaches await the traveller as well as some former inhabitants of North Africa. Wines from the Rhone are produced here. The city is inhabited by politically raucous people. The cuisine is both international and savoury. Origin of the bouillabaisse; rockfish, red mullet, scorpion fish, monkfish and crayfish. Served with croutons, aioli sauce and rouille sauce. Make the splurge for a fine reputable restaurant. Allow 24-hour notice. Then return for your prepared bouillabaisse flavorful meal of a lifetime. Be sure to enjoy a local Rhone wine with your feast. Remember you spent a lot of money to get here. So this is a worthy time and place to splurge extra money. Don't get too tipsy, hang on tight to your passport and money. Pickpockets may be waiting for you. Stay confident and alert. You will do just fine.

1913 Mediterranean Spring beaches are not yet crowded or overly fashionable. The first brush strokes of the Impressionist painters are hitting the canvas. If you can possibly afford one of the best paintings your ancestors may inherit art worth more than a million dollars. Now is the time to stock up on French wine. It may be too tasty to cellar. It is OK to indulge, you're on a cruise. Last of all recommendation. If you want to impress the folks back home purchase a French outfit and be welcome home in the latest fashion. Bon Voyage.

As more than 2,000 passengers return to the ship a buzz of excitement is in the air. The first Port of call has been a smashing success. Having been warned by the ship's attendants to carefully guard their valuables most of the travellers return unscathed. Tomorrow Barcelona is the Port of call. A European cruise aboard a new luxury liner could never be better. Anticipation is driving them forward.

It is a short cruise to Barcelona. Spain's second
largest city. The passengers of the RMS Olympic
enjoy a good night's rest before entering the next
Port of call. Many of the guests to the city stroll the
length of the wide lavish Rambla; a market
thoroughfare extends the harbour to Plaza de
Cataluna. They have left behind the cool damp
climate of London, England. Early Spring has
arrived in Barcelona. Warm sun shines down on
market oranges, peaches, grapes and almonds for
sale. Buying is robust. As they stroll further, they
stop in wonder of caged African monkeys, tropical
birds and intricate Asian animal cages for sale. No
cruise ship buyers here, just admires. The flower
shop is doing better business. Such lovely flowers,
many of them not seen in London flower shops.
The end of La Rambla opens up to the grand
inviting Plaza de Cataluna. Tourist fed pigeons
bowing their heads are there to greet them. Some
purchase bird seed and are soon surrounded by
eager feathered friends

New and old Barcelona has wondrous architecture.
1913, 20th century master designer

Antoni Guadi's Cathedral has just got started as an
architectural wonder that could be inspirational for
centuries. Barcelona is home to many beautiful

churches and Cathedrals of the Holy Cross and Saint Eulalia. The city has 15 churches and Cathedrals and is a welcoming home to Catholicism. Walk through the original old Barcelona. See remnants of the Roman wall. Watch as Joseph Oriol Mestres finishes his 1913 facade to the Barcelona Cathedral. While walking about you are advised to take a peak at restaurant menus. "I personally recommend "Los Caracoles' ', {The Snails}. The food and atmosphere are excellent here and the family staff is warm and friendly. Opened 1835.

What a great way to keep your money in your pocket. Go to the beach. March can be beautiful this time of year. Here you are before the rush of tourists arrives in April. Go get your swimsuit and towel. Take a taxi tour to hunt for the sandy beach that is most inviting to you. If you are worried about running low in funds. Skip the taxi and walk to the nearest beach. You will be as happy as a clam if you do.

The second port of call must have been as exciting as the first. The deep loud low horn sounds. The ship, crew and passengers are destined for Rome, Italy. The third and final Port destination. Rome is still the origin of Western Civilization. Roman law,

Latin language and Western Architecture have origins in Italy. If you want to know where you are going? It helps to know where you have been. This is the twentieth century. Look back. 3,000 years of history is on display today in Rome. Grab a good pair of walking shoes. Let us see what we can find.

Nearby the Roman Forum and across the street the Colosseum dating back to 500 B.C. next a 2-kilometre walk takes you to the Pantheon, the Trevi fountain and the Spanish steps. Next you want to see the Vatican then enter St. Peter's Basilica, go inside and find Bernini's bronze Baldacchino and Michael Angelo's Pieta.

Rome is a big city with many fun and exciting places to eat. If you want good budget food, try pasta or pizza dishes. Rome has excellent cuisine. Meat dishes of pork, chicken, lamb and beef are sumptuous. Fresh seafood is prepared with aromatic spices. If you are looking for a genuine Italian finale, be sure to try a frozen fruit gelato. Choices abound.

Magnifica; A vacation enjoyed to the fullest. Ten days of cruising together united the Shellhorn family. They were a unified family in each other's company. Returning to London at the end of the cruise. Each member of the family found a separate purpose. Spring break is over. Abel returned to school and his studies. Laura attended to making a home and sharing the adventures of her cruise with her bridge game ladies. Garret rushed back to Africa to tend to the mining business. Years later when Abel anguished for a year in the diamond mine he was angry with his father. However, he was forever grateful for the cruise experience of being a happy united family. Abel would get past the hate he had endured as a miner. He would even learn to respect the old Dutchman. 23-Year-old Abel worked at his father's mine and was anguished. Later given the freedom to prove himself competent in the family shipping business Abel formed a new bond with his father that suited them both well. They worked seamlessly as a business unit. They acted as father and son only as tradition required. There was never much love between the two of them before. It was money and prestige that motivated each of the men.

Chapter 3

Able Enters the Shipping Trade

It felt so good to be back in London for the Cambridge graduate. Abel had recovered from working Garett's mines A career in shipping would be infinitely more hospitable than working the diamond mines of South Africa. Abel immediately adjusted to life in London.

Dining at home my mother Laura prepared tasty home cooked stews filled with beef or chicken simmered with potatoes and carrots. I enjoy after dinner glasses of French or Spanish red wine. I often finish the evening with a small glass of Portuguese Oporto. Each morning I bathe warm and clean. Having only cold-water showers in South Africa. I appreciate my daily hot baths. My mother, Laura, is happy to have me home. My Cambridge former classmates are full of entertaining gossip. My friends are always ready for drinking and carousing. Daily my friends call me on the telephone and ask. "Able, can you join me for this or that?" Simply not having the luxury of a telephone scares me.

Then I am reminded that privilege has a price. The key to my future is to become a successful shipping merchant. I need to make an appointment or two with the fathers of my friends to see if I can generate some capital investments for the fledgling family shipping company or I will eventually run out of money. Tomorrow morning, I will return to the Cambridge University Library to research the shipping business. I must prepare a formal business plan to entice investors and appease my wary father. The old man could throw me back into the mines or have me left with no access money at all. Totally unacceptable.

My first shipping investigative research was from the British Naval Records. I took particular interest in finding the extensive loss of WWI. ships from German U-boats and sunken ships from explosions of mined harbours. How can a shipping business make money while losing such valuable ships to enemy fire? I believe reducing war damage cost will be the key to maintaining profits in a hostile world. Next, I examined individual logbooks of merchant ships. I am looking for clues to navigate perilous waters at war. Again, I noted the heavy loss of commercial vessels during World War One from the individual logs. There must be strategies that proved successful to these ships that didn't sink. Of course, the logs of the many sunken ships are unavailable for comparison.

I took stock of what tensions had resurfaced again post WWI. The German people were reuniting again under the leadership of an angry Hitler. Feared again are the dreaded German U-Boats to unleash the wolfpack submarines to the peril of modern merchant ships. How can I protect my fledgling fleet of ships? I read through the many ship's logs gleaning for information that could prove useful. I returned again and again in my thirst for knowledge. At times my heart pounds as I read. It was as if I were aboard the very ships that sailed the high seas. Sunk to the bottom or glorious in defiance full steam ahead.

Years later in the shipping business Abel would be aboard one of his company ships and conspire with the captain how other ships had overcome adversity. Abel learned from the experience of other captains to become a valued guide to running a profitable shipping business minimising war time loss. He was also convinced the knowledge gained from his research at Cambridge University was invaluable. Two weeks after extensive research

Abel felt compelled to take action. It was time to secure new investments.

I had made the acquaintance of Earnest Stanley, a distant relative from my mother's family, while attending classes at Cambridge University. Earnest's father is Lord Stanley. I telephoned Earnest and asked if he fancied meeting for a pint of ale? Earnest was a shoe in for a pint. All I had to do was ask. We met at Dragon's Lair Ale House. Conversation grew lively after we each had a second pint of Watney's ale. We talked about student friends and professors. We rekindled the shared experience of meeting French women and drinking Burgundy wines. We had met in Paris not so long ago. We talked of war and peace. Lamenting some of our friends and family had perished in the Great War. We shared our losses, then wished for peace. Peace is joyous. We both believed that mounting tensions would send Europe back into War. Peace is not at hand. War is all that is certain.

Before leaving I said. "I hate to ask. Could you get me a short appointment with your father?" Earnest responded. "You dog you. Sure I can get you my old man's ear if you need it? Thanks Earnest we will have to do this again. It has been great talking to you, Able. I will see you later." Both young men knew as they departed one or both of them could die in the fighting that was certain to follow.

Before meeting with Lord Stanley, I donned my best attire. I wore fine woollen grey slacks with a matching vest and long tailed coat. I arrived at the Lord Stanley Manor driven by a London taxi at a quarter to nine as requested. I was greeted by a staff member and ushered into Lord Stanley's private library. The wood panels and furniture are sturdy and lavish. The library's collection is extensive. Many of the books are rare collectables, some dating back 600 years. The library is divided into separate sections International Affairs, Military Campaigns, Common Law, Commerce and politics. The library has collections in English and Latin. Lord Stanley is Able's third cousin. Able's mother was too modest to make the connection. They shared a great-great grandfather of his mother. Stanley walked in then offered me a glass of Scotch Whiskey. He poured a half-poured glass into a heavy crystal. Lord Stanley cut straight to business. "What is it you want from me Able?" The two men had never spoken before, and I was set off guard by Lord Stanley's abruptness. Stanley chuckled and spoke. "You will have to excuse me.

It seems I spend most of the day working with people in crisis mode. Please let's start over. :Earnest tells me. You are a good man to have a pint with. Scotch is my choice of drink. You are drinking my favourite Scotch. I personally brought it back from Scotland. Of course, the best fun comes from the sampling of various Scotch Blends while in Scotland. Now you tell me something I don't know about yourself. I have never had this kind of Scotch Whiskey before, I like it." Replied Able. Lord Stanley said. "Pretend I am just Earnest's father and not a Conservative Lord of Parliament. It would do me a world of good to converse like an ordinary man." Stanley called in a staff member and told him. "Alex, please reschedule my next appointment until tomorrow." I was very careful to not ask for any commitments that evening. I was given the chance to explore my aspiration of leasing ships in war time. Stanley was astute knowing that was the reason for his appointment. His son Earnest had tipped him off. Lord Stanley was a Cambridge man too. What fun it was to share experiences as students with a couple of his oldest professors. Abel left smiling and happy. Cheerfully Stanley commented. "I will consider your lease proposal, Able. Have yourself a good evening." Abel felt he was walking on air as he strolled along Barclay Square in London. Having access to top political leaders could prove very useful.

The following week I received a telegram from Lord Stanley. I read Stanley's telegram.

I, feeling enthused, sprang into action. This was
better than I could even dream of. I had hoped to
find an investor or two to defer the great cost of
acquiring new ships. Now that it was certain the
world was destined for another deadly war, The
Shellhorn shipping company would need to protect
itself from the losses of war. Leasing ships in war
waters is infinitely more attractive than having your

ownership investments sink to the bottom of the sea. I will travel to America tomorrow on the first ship available destined for New York.

There was no sleeping tonight. I spent the evening packing and preparing a written agenda. My plan for action. London is the shipping capital of the world. Certainly, I could jump aboard a ship to America in the morning.

It was no easy task finding passage to New York on such short notice. Fortune had it that a ship could always squeeze one more passenger in 3rd class, deck side. It took till evening. I shouldered my duffel bag aboard The Constellation, a tried-and-true older passenger ship. The sun rose from the horizon on departure. I stretched out on a deck bench covered in a complementary ship's rug. I slept with the angels then awakened to a glorious sunrise. "I feel hungry as hell." Abel announced it to the world. I am ready to find breakfast and I am famished. I ate sunny fried eggs served with toast and orange marmalade all washed down with Royal Queen's tea. I felt renewed as the Constellation travelled West to America. She was making 16 knots which was more than adequate for her 40-year-old hull. I breathed in the freshly salted air. I was destined for New York city. It was a dream come true. The United States of America held promises that I did not have at home. I was going to set foot onto a land with people that had thumbed their nose at the English Royal Crown in 1776. The power of the British Navy and the commerce of the English Crown ruled much of the 18th century world. Yet a ragtag bunch of yankee rebels declared their declaration of independence in 1776. Even more astonishing in a few short years they formed a new constitutional government.

I am a contemporary traveller that fancied the American rebel spirit. England like America prospered best led by elected leaders that are held accountable to the tax paying citizens. Both countries are democracies. I knew that when I got to America, I would have serious work to do to secure ship leasing contracts. I first planned to enter the ship building yards to learn more about the new Liberty ships being manufactured, then I would need to explore political connections to secure lease options. The thought that Liberty ships were reserved for exclusive American patriots never crossed my mind.

Abel Shellhorn gazed upon the statue, appreciating her beauty. She looked back at him revealing a softened Romanesque face. Abel instantly recognized a dignified confidence, almost a regal quality. The statue before him was created by Alexandre-Emmanuel the French designer of the

Eiffel Tower. The Liberty Statue is modelled after the artist's own mother. Seeing the inspirational monument entering the gateway harbour to New York inspired Able. Greatness lay ahead in America. Many of the other ship's passengers too were lost in the grandeur and promise of America. The new day felt glorious.

I got off the ship, my travel bag in hand and shoulder. A caravan of Yellow Cab & Checker Taxis welcomed the ship's passengers to the sights and sounds of New York City. I pulled my stuff into the closest available car and directed the driver. "Please take me to the shipyard building the new Liberty ships." The driver was very familiar with the ship construction sites. I asked. "If possible, take me to a nearby place of lodging, after I get a view of the shipyard location." Soon I was checked into a clean and secure hotel room. After a short walkabout I determined this location would work nicely. I returned to my hotel room, kicked off my shoes and closed my eyes momentarily. I had no idea when I last had a good night's sleep. I slept for many hours. It was the next evening when I woke up. I left my room and soon I found the finest restaurant in town preparing the famous New York Charcoal Grilled Ambassador Steak. With a fork and knife I cut into 2 inches thick one pound of medium rare cooked top loin beef. Glorious.

Enjoying the meal with a 7-year-old fifth of 1932 French Chateau Latour Grand Vin Bordeaux is stupendous. A fine restaurant like this had plenty of eye candy. Pretty girls, lovely dresses, women with jewels and sophistication. "Just enjoy yourself old boy. You will make time to entertain the fancy of an American girl." For the traveller of a great international city like New York City. Anything you can imagine can be found. If you know how to find it.

The following day I was work ready for the Liberty Ship Yard. I wore a scruffy pair of dark denim pants and a light-coloured short sleeve shirt. The morning started with 62 degrees of Spring sunshine. I am ready to work a hard day of labour. There is no need to apply for work. My job is to gain knowledge. Soon enough if all goes well I will be paid negotiating a leasing contract that will profit me plenty. 6:45 A.M The job site is crawling with men glad to do a day's work. I casually walk into the work site, then find my chance to lend a hand. The smell of burnt metal welded in sheets of steel, greased rails and iron permeate the air. I found work as a day labourer supplying material to some 600 feet of ship's hull being assembled. Iron is heavy stuff. I find I'm using muscles not used in the sport of collegiate tennis. Soon my arms ache, perhaps past pick and shovel work in South African mines is helping me keep up with the other workers.

My real goal is to find a chance to learn some inside information from the supervisory staff. Which means I need to make contact with the supervisors without appearing to be a brown nose threat to the other workers. This is a work crew of tough men. Some that certainly have reputations of tearing a guy's head off in a fight. I am constantly watching as I work. I noticed that a few of the workers are frequently running between various men with clipboards. I look for opportunities. I got the chance and stole a clipboard. Fortunately I wore a comfortable light weight shoe today. If one of the iron rails fell on these flimsy shoes I would be sure to break some toes. I take the risk of standing out as I change job stations.

When I thought I could make a break for it I made a run for a supervisor standing with a clipboard. I stopped in front of this target, then waited. This man bellowed at me. "What the hell are you just standing there for!? Grab a box and take it over there." He pointed to the location to go, and I was off and running. This runner's job was much more akin to tennis, as . I compared this ship's previous labour iron supplier job to that of working in the diamond mine.

I was proud as hell. One hour working in the shipyard and I already was promoted. Working directly with supervisors I was permitted occasional breaks and gained the scuttlebutt of the Liberty ship business. I continued to work each day at the shipyard gaining knowledge. I learned that Franklin Delano Roosevelt was a great fan of the liberty ship program. Politically the President was doing everything possible to expand production. They had immediate plans to expand in other shipyards along the East Coast. Furthermore, plans for Liberty ship production were under way for the West coast of the United States as well.

While running from station to station I noticed a man with an Argus C3 camera repeatedly changing lenses and photographing the ship's construction in various stages. The man's name is Bob Hansen. I was informed by a supervisor that Mr. Hansen is a friend of President Rosevelt. He is here on a mission to document the progress of the first of many Liberty ships to be built in America. Armed with this information I boldly intercepted Mr. Hansen at the end of his work shift. I called out to the photographer. "You and I have something in common. We are both here doing investigative research on the production of this Liberty Ship." I approached the camera man and extended my hand in friendship. "My name is Abel Shellhorn. I am the managerial owner of Shellhorn Shipping Company. I like what I see here. I am very interested in investment purchases of ships like these. Bob Hansen replied. "It is still too early to hash out the details. Please take my business card. Give me a call this evening and I will see if we can set something up. I thanked him for the card and promised to call this evening. I was feeling very lucky.

Later That evening I telephoned Mr Bob. Hansen and made arrangements to meet in Hyde Park at the 1939 World's Fair held at Flushing Meadows. I was told that Bob Hansen would have someone there that would be fun to meet. I had no idea who the mystery guest would be. I was thinking, a pretty American girl could be fun to meet. I was in for a very big surprise.

I made my way through the long line of New York Fair attendees. All the time thinking how will I ever find Bob Hansen in this humongous crowd? It appeared all of New York City was here at the Park. Ahead of me a festive band sprang to life. Festooned in a red, white and blue hat stood President Franklin Deleno Roosevelt. Standing next to him was Bob Hansen, smirking happily. He was looking for Able. Sure enough Abel stood out in a state of shock. Bob took notice and hollered out. "Able, come over here and meet the President.

I told Franklin you want to buy some of his boats."
President Roosevelt addressed Able. "This is a
political campaign. Nod your head and smile a lot.
If you do that well I will have you an appointment
set for Monday. Now smile."

I could never in a million years plan such a
successful launch into America's high society. The
whole time with the presidential entourage I Smiled
and smiled some more. I didn't eat, drink or talk. I
did as I was told. Photographs of the president and
his guest were constantly being taken. The next
day I would learn I was the mystery man. No one in
all of New York fathomed the Identity of Abel
Shellhorn. All they knew is that he had a winning
smile. Bob Hansen and Franklin D. Roosevelt
Knew who Abel Shellhorn is and they are NOT
talking.

Bob Hansen telephoned Abel later that night. He
spoke. "You did well, Able. You followed Franklin's
direction to a T. The President is very impressed. A
background check is being done on you now." We
will need to get some personal data on you and the
Shellhorn Shipping business. By the end of next
week if everything checks out you can go to the
press with a photo op. And a ship's purchase
agreement. Welcome to New York City Democratic
Politics! That does it. Shellhorn shipping has a new
future in America.

Chapter 4

Kate

Kate is a climber. At the age of 6 months Kate scooted around the Stanley home on well-trodden knees. Suddenly it occurred to Kate she could improve her outlook by hoisting herself upright with the aid of the sofa. Kate found this to be a fun new challenge. Soon Kate was finding new and interesting things to climb or not to climb.

Kate's mother Beatrice is on the constant lookout to keep her daughter a safe climber and their precious glass treasures from being smashed by probing hands. Being the mom of a young child and managing a home can be exhausting. Kate is a lucky girl to have a dad that comes home from work and is ready to give mom a break and entertain his daughter.

Kate's dad, Russel Stanley works at the Bank of England. It is his job to work with finances and people all day long. He looks forward each day to coming home where he doesn't have to worry about money. The first thing Russ does is to greet his 6-month-old daughter Kate then develop a game or activity to play with her. Today Russ added a chair and a box for Kate to discover and if she chooses, she can add them to her climbing expedition.

Three full months go by before, 9 months old, Kate transcends to walking upright. Even then Kate occasionally fondly clings to the arm of the couch or a chair.

 Autumn days delight 3-year-old Kate the climber. Russ invites his wife and daughter out for raked leaves adventures. First they rake the leaves into a tall mountain high pile. Then Bea and Russ take turns hiding in the piles. Soon Kate discovers she too can hide amongst the leaves. Kate's favourite leaf game is claw climbing to the mountain top then declaring herself Queen of the mountain. As the days, weeks and months go by she enjoys many game choices. The Stanleys love to play games.

Age 7 Kate has grown up with a backyard London Plane tree. The 14-year-old tree was planted in the Springtime to celebrate Kate's birth. The tree and her grew up together. Alone in her yard she sized the tree up. She knew every branch and every twig.

Today she would climb that tree. She would have to be very careful not to break any branches. It was dad's favourite tree. He had planted this tree when it was 8 feet tall. Today the tree neared 20 feet in height far smaller than the giant oak tree that towered near the house.

Russel came home from the Bank of England. He was tired and mildly stressed. He grabbed a cold beer then plopped onto the sofa. Kate walked in her house then gagged her dad's mood She said, "Daddy can you come outside to see what I can do? Yes." He replied. He found it difficult to tell her no. Kate had been successful climbing the tree earlier in the day. Now she had an audience who was also protective of his tree.

Kate began to climb. Sturdy lower scaffold branches are perfect for hand over hand hoisting into the canopy. Soon she has her feet positioned for her climb up. She studies her options. Previously Kate had ascended on the right side of the canopy. Now she could see an alternate route inside the left canopy. Maybe she would try the left assent later. She would stick with the same tried and true climb she had made earlier. After a quick confident climb Kate's feet were perched on a branch high enough up for Kate to poke her head atop the tree's canopy. Kate hollered out. "Hello down there daddy." Russ replied. "You be careful climbing down." Much to Kate's surprise. Her daddy quietly hoisted himself into the tree canopy. Before climbing down to the ground, they each sat and chatted about her day.

13-year-old Kate sat in the Stanley family car. A short drive later and they will be in London's Hyde Park to attend the annual Stanley reunion. They will all gather for Picnic foods and beverages later in the day. The adults mill about cajoling and gossiping. While some of the youths drift into the park looking for adventure or mischief.

Kate finds boys intriguing. They are certainly different from girls. Kate spies 17-year-olds Abel and Earnest drifting away from the reunion. She follows behind unknown. Out of sight Earnest produces a package of cigarettes. The two teenagers sit on a log to smoke. Kate approaches the boys and asks. "Would you like to see me climb that tree over there?" Kate pointed to a tree. Earnest was quick to say. "Yeah." Kate looked right at Able, smiled then ran to her tree thinking. Abel is interesting. His mother is Stanley. His South African Dutch father, Garret is a Shellhorn and rumored to be rich. How is that?

Kate chose a tree that is a challenging climb to begin with but easy for her to climb once secure in the canopy. Her entry branch is a good 7 feet off of the ground. Completely focused Kate made a running hop then two-handed grasp and hoist. Pulling her body up the tree then climbing with her feet up into the tree until she grasped upper branches then secured her footing on the lower branch. Kate focused on climbing into the 60-foot-tall tree. Earnest turned to Stanley and exclaimed. "I was going to bet you a sterling pound she would never get off the ground." Now both of the boys worried for her safety. Kate made it look easy climbing the tree. She is as careful going up as she is going down. Finale. Her feet dangle two feet above the ground. She easily makes the hop down. Earnest and Abel run to congratulate her on a tremendous climb. Both boys are quietly relieved nothing went wrong.

 5 Years after the Stanley family reunion Kate and Abel would meet again in America. The daring skinny 13-year-old tree climber blossomed into an 18 year old mature self-confident and attractive lady. The 23-year-old Abel had resumed the family name of Shellhorn. He worked an arduous year in his father's South African mine. This earned his father Garret Shellhorn's trust and employment management of the fledgling Shellhorn Shipping Company. America invites opportunity for those that seek it.

Kate and Abel both have set foot in America knowing nothing of the other adult lives. As Abel approaches his hotel room, he is greeted by a young boy clad in a grey Western Union uniform. The boy smiled from under his company hat. Then he inquired. "Are you Mr. Abel Shellhorn? Indeed I Am." The lad handed him a telegram. I thanked him and handed him a 10 cent tip. He thanked me and left me wondering what news had come my way. I entered my room to inquire.

The telegraph read. "Cousin Kate arrives in New York 11-21 please greet her at noon RMS Olympic docking." Mum

The next day Abel joined the bustling crowd that stood waiting for the arrival of the RMS Olympic. As the passengers disembarked, he held the Stanley sign high above his head. Cousin Kate did see the STANLEY sign and pulled her escort close to her to meet her cousin. She was escorted shoreside by Alphonso. Kate approached Able. She recognized the older Abel from photographs taken at Stanley family gatherings. Abel politely kissed her on the cheek. "Welcome to New York." His last memory of Kate was that of a young venturous girl climbing a tall tree in Hyde Park . Now standing in front of him was a shapely model working for Revlon Nails with an auburn-haired doll face. Her escort sported a thin diamond studded gold wedding band. His face featured a Roman nose perched above a pierced grimace face. Alphonso's sportsmen's green eyes focused on Abel as he extended his hand to Able. Abel evaluated the man; he was careful not to pass judgement. He ignored his extended hand. He had the feeling this man could spell trouble for Kate. There were no rings worn on Kate's fingers Before the two of them left for the city Abel pressed a business card into Kate's hand and whispered into her ear. "Please stay in touch with me Kate." Abel wondered if. "Would he ever see her again?"

Before the 1939 German bombs fell from London's sky the people of this great city enjoyed life as it should be. Love and idle conversation. Family picnics, theatre, dancing and sports. All that changed during World War Two. Food was rationed. People readied to dive into bomb shelters or join the fight often in some distant land. Abel left his homeland to help the Great War efforts supplying American Liberty Ships to bring war supplies and troops to anywhere a ship could venture to. Now the War was bringing the two Stanley cousins together in America.

Kate's ticket to America was presented by Alphonso at a London nightclub; he would be her ticket out of town, away from the fear of constant bombing and hours of boredom cooped up at home. Alphonso travelled to London as a purchasing agent. He worked for Revlon cosmetics. America was free of war in 1939. Revlon needed European products. He worked in London to procure European beauty products that could be sold at the New York Selfridge Department store. There could be no harm in a little entertainment after work. Acquainting with pretty women, some eager to escape the German bombardment. Alphonso felt he wasn't a target being Italian American he was well acquainted with both sides of the War.

Alphonso, who had an appreciation for young attractive women, was always looking for an opportunity to extend a career opportunity in exchange for friendship. Kate was his target. Alphonso secreted his wedding ring out of sight. Mustering all his charm he approached her, smiled, then asked. "Would you like to come with me, then work as a sales rep. In the world's greatest Department Store?" Kate could scarcely believe her ears. Alphonso went on to tell Kate all the wonders of the New York Selfridge Department store. He concluded his spiel. "I am Alphonso Lucini, Revlon's top salesman." He then handed her his professional calling card then offered to find her work in New York working at the Selfridge Department Store. Kate simply couldn't say no.

The ship was leaving tomorrow morning at 8:00 A.M. Kate threw a change of clothes and her personal essentials into a handbag then awakened her mother Beatrice to excitedly share the news of a hasty departure to a safe refuge in America.

Fortunately, the next morning Alphonso was waiting at the dock way to the ship with her tickets in his hand. It would be an interesting crossing of the Atlantic Ocean with her newfound friend. Kate had her work cut out for her. She had no intention of sleeping with this guy in exchange for her passage to America. If tensions got to be too much, she was prepared to pay him for her ship's passage. The first rule Kate insisted. She would pay for her own meals. She chose cheap fare for meals. She skipped some meals to save money. She politely invited Alphonso to accompany lunch paying Dutch. Initially Alphonso made it a challenge to bed her in his luxurious room aboard the ship. Insisting. "You must come see the lavish room the Revlon company paid for." By the end of the cruise, he failed to even show Kate the splendour of his accommodations. Kate was a tough nut to crack. She did have a winning smile and was pleasurable to talk with. Alphonso wasn't a fool. She would get a sales job working the Revlon Cosmetics Counter at Selfridges New York Department Store as promised. Kate Would be responsible to make an acceptable sales commission to keep her job. Alphonso was careful to place his wedding band back on when they arrived in New York. He would not like his wife jumping to any ill-humoredly conclusions.

Kate busied herself learning the products and sales at the Cosmetic counter of Selfridge Department store After one year of service she was the top salesclerk with perfect attendance. She was awarded the title as the new Sales Manager for her efforts. Many of Selfridges department managers needed 5 years of service or more to be promoted to the ranks of management. Rumours started. " She is just a flirt. Who did she sleep with to get the job?" Who is she related to?" Some of the workers accepted that she earned her managerial promotion. Others did not.

Most of the ladies working at the Cosmetic Counter liked working with Kate. Kate made the work schedules and did employee evaluations. It is prudent and profitable to stay on Kate's good side .Kate ignored the gossipers and did her job well. Kate quite possibly would still be working somewhere in a New York Department Store had the incident not occurred.

Alphonso Lucine has two employers. Revlon Cosmetics and Selfridge Department Store. The

Selfridge store employs Mr. Lucine to be the sole source of Revlon products in the exclusive Revlon Counter residing in the Selfridge store. Alphonso's job is a very busy endeavour. He shops the world for new products. When he is in New York he meets with other product representatives and promotes new cosmetics to the sales staff of the Selfridge Cosmetic Counter. Alphonso is an elegantly dressed man whose charming smile has greeted many of the women who work here. It is no wonder rumours of him fly about like bees from a disturbed nest. Alphonso married a woman of striking beauty adorned with the latest fashions. Little of his wife is known.

The Cosmetic Counter has a small break room. A few chairs, a short sofa and a table is all. The break room doubles as a private locking conference room door. Only managers have keys to the conference room. Privacy is expected when the door is locked.

It is just another day as usual at Selfridges. That is until Kate watches Mr. Lucini escort a lady into the conference room. She was close enough to the door to hear the metallic sound of the door being locked. Kate stood directly outside the door, holding her breath, listening. She has no idea what

is happening in the room. She listens thinking if it
was me that man is forcing himself on I would want
intervention, Kate waited a few minutes then quietly
inserted her kay to unlock the door. So as not to be
alarming she stealthily entered the dimmed room to
investigate. What she saw was shocking. The
Lucinis were coupled and entwined naked on the
sofa. Their clothes were abandoned then strewn in
a heap on the floor. A crimson red Kate had made
a big mistake. She knew she had to apologise and
stand her ground. Mr. Lucine spoke first. Kate I can
explain. First we need 5 minutes to get organised.
"May I suggest that you lock the door on your way
out, then return in a few minutes to discuss what
you saw here and what your future employment
might be.

A few minutes later Kate entered the break room.
The door was unlocked. The Lucine couple had
laid naked in dignified contentment. In a New York
minute their strewn clothes had found their
masters. Alphonso was ready to defend his family
honour. He began. "Kate, I suggest you saw
nothing out of the ordinary when you entered this
room. Rumours will circulate as they always do." I
am prepared to offer you two weeks' severance
pay and the guarantee of a fresh start employed in
a West Coast Department store. Of course, we will
pay for your travel expenses. All I require from you

is a simple YES, we are in agreement. We face the predicament of both staying here and suffering the consequences. This won't be the first time or the last time such arrangements from the galivanting Alphonso. Kate agreed to the terms of her departure. She grabbed her purse and headed home.

The following day Alphonso approached the Cosmetic Counter to share the good news Kate has been offered a new exciting job at the San Francisco West.Coast Emporium Department Store. She will be working in the same city as her older cousin Able. She will continue working for the Revlon Company.

Monday morning Kate boarded the transcontinental business class train for San Francisco, California. This steam powered world class train claims to make the trip across the country from New York in 83 hours. Kate telegraphed Abel to meet her at the San Francisco Train Station at the daily arrival time of 7:00 AM. Thursday.

Chapter 5

Fresh Start

Who would have thought Abel Shellhorn who had recently survived the hellish Shellhorn diamond mind in wretched darkness and surviving the dangerous conditions. Would be resurrected to rub elbows with aristocrats. Abel feels secure in a New York taxicab destined to dine on Thanksgiving Day with Bob Hansen, a confidant of President Franklin Delanor Roosevelt. Abel Shellhorn made a lifelong pledge. "I will forever remain a humble benefactor to this change in circumstances." Abel remained true to his pledge. Years later when he retired from day-to-day work, he credits this simple oath as what brought him many riches. Abel is best known as a man of quiet determination. The Shellhorn clan could be tough bastards, the bunch of them never forgot their loyalties. Never.

Bob Hansen likes to have fun. He makes a living out of making friends and associates that get things done. He truly knows the people who know President Franklin Delanor Roosevelt. That is why Franklin hired Bob to be on his team. Robert Bob Hansen was born a Democrat. No. He is not a tax and spend Democrat. He is a Capital Investment man. He and the President find there is nothing more exciting than the prospects of a New Deal. It is no surprise Bob lives in a 7-bedroom apartment residing on 5th Avenue that features a stunning view of New York Central Park. Bob considers it his mission in life to keep the 5th Avenue residence a hopping bunch of loyalists circulating and promoting Democratic Party ideals. This is exactly why Abel Shellhorn is being brought into the fold. Abel Shellhorn has potential. If they are not careful, a guy like him could become a Republican. Perhaps lost forever.

The fact is all governments tax and spend. The real question is. Do they tax equitably and provide needed services fairly and efficiently?

After a sumptuous Thanksgiving meal of rib roast beef, foul and stuffing and potatoes served from a pastry bag. Red wine from the French Bordeaux and Rhone regions are served with the beef and the pheasant. The wine glasses are never allowed to empty until the bottles are emptied. After the table was cleared of plates Bob invited any who appreciated cigars and cognac to be served in the library. I was surprised to see a young lady with her hair styled short and fashionable join us men in the library. I noticed Bob seemed to be pleased.

Bob worked the room engaging in small conversation, taking the time to keep the cognac glasses from running empty. He is a masterful host. The mood of the room remains upbeat. It appeared Jane, the single lady that entered with the smoking men, seemed to focus her attention on Bob. The other men were polite to Jane but seemed to basically pay little attention to her. Eventually Bob sat next to me to converse. The first thing that he said to me. "Able. I spoke to President Roosevelt." "He said, 'I like Able. I would like to bring him aboard.' You Know, Able. You don't argue with the President of the United States of America. Especially if he is a Roosevelt." I dropped my jaw open in disbelief.

Jane had been listening to Bob. She got up, crossed the room, and sat next to Bob. Bob introduced her to me as a good friend of his. She said, "We think you will be a great part of the Democratic ticket."

Bob chimed in. "We would like to offer you the opportunity to stay here with us in New York. You can stay here for free while you build your shipping company."

I of course said, "Yes," and many, "Thank you."

No contract was signed. Nothing was written in blood. I gave my word. Through thick and thin the allegiance has always held.

It is after nine o'clock at night. President Franklin Delano Roosevelt arrived in his personal hand driven Ford Phaeton custom motor car. He had driven over 90 miles from the affluent Hyde Park in Upstate New York. His polio-stricken feet never touched the pedals in the 3-hour-plus drive here. The clever man engineered himself hand levers to operate the car by hands only. As per agreement, Bob and I quietly lifted him into the house. We then set up a small table and his personal chair. Before guests and staff were allowed into the parlour, Franklin was provided a fleece blanket to cover his legs and dignify his appearance. FDR enjoys bartending his own drinks as well as others. He typically chooses either whiskey for Old Fashions or gin martinis shaken with a light touch of vermouth. Tonight, he chose rum from the Virgin Islands and added brown sugar and orange juice.

The Roosevelt court is ready to be in session or as FDR Called "The Children's Hour".

The first person Abel knew by name was Kate Stanley, his second cousin to greet the President. There are easily a dozen people before her excited to welcome FDR. Most walked away with a presidential-crafted cocktail. I noticed as Franklin talked and poured inconsistencies at his craft. Some are poured stronger; some are poured weaker. No matter. The President of the United States is taking the time to connect with the guests on a personal level. I eavesdropped on the conversation Kate had with FDR. Roosevelt told her. "Bob Hansen thought Abel and Kate could make a nice couple." Kate turned scarlet red and excused herself from the President. I couldn't help but laugh. Later in the evening, I noticed she looked beautiful in her long black formal dress. Late into the evening, the visitors disappeared into the night. The remaining residents retired to their rooms. FDR was not to be seen. Bob told me. "Franklin stays in the best room in the house. We certainly wouldn't want him driving home at this hour. We helped him get situated about a half hour ago."

Abel is the first of Bob Hansen's guests to awake to a new day. The domestic help had already prepared coffee, tea, hot cocoa, and a tray of fresh pastries. Fresh fruit and juice were also available. Abel sipped and snacked, then grabbed an apple. Abel left smiling and thinking. "Now I know why Bob always has a god damn big smile on his face."

Chapter 6

The Un-wedding

Abel Shellhorn nervously paced back and forth outside the grand entry of Selfridge Department Store. How would he ask Katharine Bea Stanley for her hand in holy matrimony?

Summoning courage, Abel steadfastly marched to the Revlon Cosmetic Department, where Selfridges newest department manager, Kate, was busily working at the sales counter. He waits until she is momentarily free. Then asks her. "Is there any place we can go to talk in private?"

Kate replied. "Please give me a minute to have another salesclerk cover for me, then we can meet in private in the conference room."

Kate wondered. "What could be so important for him to interrupt me at work?"

Kate unlocked the door to the conference room. Abel opened the door, then the two of them entered. Kate instinctively locked the door. Abel did say. "We meet in private." Abel kneeled at her feet and offered her a felt jewelry box. Kate is not at all confident about how this will play out. She waits for Abel to speak. "My dear Kate, I ask for your hand in marriage? I know this is a bit of a surprise. I have always found you desirable and attractive." Abel opened the jewelry box revealing to Kate a most magnificent wedding ring. The band is made from rare white gold. The large 3-carat diamond is nestled in a delicate yellow 14-carat golden nest. The fine South African gemstone captured the light in the room and then shone into wide-open eyes of Katherine.

Kate instinctively reaches out to pull her gift closer. For a moment, all she can think is. "I must marry this love-struck prince." Abel seeing the sparkle in Kate's eyes, asks. "So, what do you think?" Kate thought beyond the moment. "What will become of her career? What will life be like living with this man?" She replied. "It all seems so fast. Should we be rushing into this?" Abel could see that Kate would not be easily swept off her feet. Abel suggested they meet for coffee across the street at the diner. They both planned to meet shortly after 7:00 PM.

Abel found a table for 2 in the diner and waited for Kate to arrive. Soon Kate came to join him. Abel marvelled at how desirable she looked. Even though her face was tired looking, and her makeup could use refreshing. So, this is what being in love must feel like. But, of course, he would have to be entirely honest with Kate.

"Kate, I need to be entirely honest with you." Thus began a lengthy discussion. "What is life to be like living as a married couple?" Abel explained to Kate to be a shipping benefactor of the FDR administration, he would need to gain American citizenship and be a settled, married man. Bob Hansen could see that Kate could be the key to all this coming together. Franklin Roosevelt agreed to sign off on this. Listening to Abel talk. Kate understood FDR's embarrassing implicit marriage comment he made at Bob Hansen's house. The two new lovers talked and talked for hours. Finally, they agreed to a simple Justice of the Peace marriage. They will have the rest of their lives to see what becomes of it. First things first, Abel suggested. "Why don't we share the good news with Bob Hansen.

Bob Hansen opened the door to his home on 5th Avenue, surprised and delighted to see the rosy-cheeked couple standing door side on a brisk March evening. Bob asked Able. "What brings you along with such a lovely escort?" Abel stammered slightly. "We're getting married." Bob asked. How so, and when? Both replied. "Tomorrow at 11:00 AM." That means I have only an hour or two to gather for a celebration party. Not to worry, I have met with success on tighter constraints. Do come inside!

10:00 PM

The house is rockin'. Abel and Kate were the only two people not dressed entirely in black. The black attire is attributed to Bob Hansen's sense of humor. There was enough booze to float a small boat, Whiskey, Gin, Champagne, and Ale. Bill even managed to snag a saxophone player to get things swinging. The house was elbow to elbow populated thickly, some dancing, most just talking. Kate and I were the celebrated couple. Early in the morning, Kate and I shared a bed together. We were way too tired to do anything but just sleep.

Before exchanging our wedding vows, we need 2 witnesses to appear before the judge. Bill, of course, vouched for me. So, what to do for Kate? Fortunately, Kate had made friends with a party guest she formerly had been acquainted with. Her name was Isabelle. Isabelle made it through the night without sleep. Being the trooper she is, she made it just fine as a witness.

The 4 of us entered the New York Courthouse. Today Judge Jack Johnson was presiding. We learned. We needed to stand in the 11:00 AM line and wait our turn. You should get in that line if you ever want to experience a cross-section of New York lives. You are likely to meet every kind of person for better or worse than one could possibly imagine. Lively conversations fired back and forth like bullets in a war battle. The listener could learn many reasons to tie the knot and be hitched appropriately.

1:05 PM.

It is our turn. Judge Jack Johnson is a colorful man to behold. Blush complexion, sailor-thickened skin, a hint of whiskey on the breath, good to mellow the exhalation of a chain-smoking saint. Jack is good at what he does. He implores the bride and groom to examine each other's soul and commit to a lasting union. Kate and Abel witnessed many matrimonial unions and will be guests to many more. Large fancy gatherings have their place. Only ongoing commitment keeps a couple together. But, through thick and thin, Kate and Abel stick together. After the pronouncement of man and wife, the 4 of us enjoyed lunch next door at Joey's. We each selected a festive sausage sandwich wrapped in a bun. Bill paid for lunch. Joey brought out an ice-cold pitcher of Budweiser beer, wishing. "I wish you a very happy marriage." Nice.

March 31, 1941. After lunch, we leisurely walked in Central Park. Conversations are light and pleasant. A rare warm 72-degree spring day pushing up tulips amongst yellow daffodils. Mostly blue sky with the last threat of Winter storm clouds fading. People are at war or planning for it everywhere in this country and throughout the world. The wedding party enjoys a brief break from the threat of war, marching to the island shores of America.

A few months later, America was under attack after Japan attacked Pearl Harbor, the Hawaiian Naval Base. Finally, on December 7, Franklin Delano Roosevelt declared war on Japan with the full backing of Congress.

The Axis powers of Germany, Italy, and Japan united within a week to declare war on the United States. The 6 years and one-day battle of WWII just got more significant with the entry of the United States of America.

Before the Declaration of WWII, President Roosevelt met Churchill and supported the war effort. Yet when Roosevelt ran for his successful re-election, he promised support in armaments promising to keep American soldiers at home. This was welcome by the popular vote. However, after the attack on Pearl Harbor, popular attitudes shifted to avenging the war against Japan and Germany.

Chapter 7

Go West

Kate Invites Abel over to spend a night at her place. When Abel arrives, he discovers Kate's Home is just a tiny room with a bed. Other than a hot plate, there is no kitchen. The bathroom is a shared locking room down the hall. Nevertheless, the place is neat and tidy.

The newly married couple ventures out for Chinese takeout. Abel insists on buying a celebratory bottle of Champagne. Back in Kate's room, a hasty meal is enjoyed. Both Abel and Kate are eager to consummate the wedding. Morning breakfast consisted of a shared orange and the last of the Champagne. Little did they know. Allen would be born 9 months later to the day. Kate's breakfast topic. "I plan to travel West later by train. I need a few weeks to organize and pack." Kate did not want to travel West in a 2 door Coupe with two young men, even though she is married to one of them now.

Abel threw his duffel bag containing his worldly possessions into the trunk of the new 1941 burgundy Plymouth coupe. Unfortunately, the trunk was already nearly full of Bob Hansen's belongings. Bob grabbed two-quart bottles of beer and hollered, "Let's go!"

I hopped in, took a swig of beer, then asked. "How could you afford this nice car?"

"I can't. Dad paid $980 for this 84-horse powered beauty with a 3 speed six-cylinder power terrain. We are driving it to the Seattle Boeing manufacturing site. Dad engineers airplanes. We are doing him a favor."

Abel replied. "This will be a fun favor to do."

The summertime pre-war drive across the country is a wake-up call to the two young men. Far from the prosperous streets of New York City, the nation is bogged down in impoverished farmland and struggling small towns and cities. The route they chose to drive is known as The Lincoln Highway, connecting the East Coast of New York to the West Coast of San Francisco. This is America's first named road to connect the two Coasts of America.

Fittingly it is named in honor of President Abraham Lincoln. If you envision a direct paved route, you are totally wrong. Bob and Abel traveled in 1941. Much of the route is unpaved and dusty.

To complete their journey, Bob drove while Abel navigated with the many maps they purchased. When they reached the Midwest, they discovered it was best to proceed with clear heads. They waited till evening to drink more alcohol. The coastal drive passes through 1500+ towns and cities, many with traffic cop speed traps. They learned to slow down, especially in the rural outskirts of town. Bob concluded that some of these traffic cops saw a new fancy car that might be the key to enriching the local economy. 10 days into the road trip, they parked the coupe at El Rancho Las Vegas Hotel. The parking lot was built in 1940 to hold 500 cars. The place was hopping.

Bob asked Able. "Shall we go check this place out for a splurge? That would be righteous." They agreed to budget their dollars but stayed the night. Swimming pool, gardens, parks, and restaurants to enjoy, but they stayed out of the Casino. They couldn't afford to gamble. They drive North to Idaho the following day, leaving behind the Lincoln Highway. They're on their own mapping the final drive to Seattle, Washington.

Two years of economic depression and dust bowl droughts take a toll on many Americans. The traveling pair are not fat cats staying nightly in fancy hotels. Instead, they find quiet places to park and sleep briefly along the westward roads. They buy snack food and beer to keep their spirits bright. Taking turns, they always keep their eyes safeguarding the Plymouth coupe. Travel is often as slow as 30 mph on unpaved roads. Occasionally they drive a straight length of good pavement. Finally, Bob shifts the coupe into 3rd gear and flies at 60 to 70 mph.

Bob and Abel rolled into Seattle, completing the first 2 weeks of their California destination. The new car has been a total champ. Other Than a thick layer of dust and road grit, the car looks and runs perfectly. They drive towards Elliott Bay. Soon they saw the Boeing Airport and completed the production of Several B-17 "Flying Fortresses." They are parked near the runway. They proceed to the largest hangar among many.

"This is where we will find Dad," said Bob. Sure enough, Bob took off to greet his dad when they walked inside.

The first thing Bob's dad said was. "Let me see my new car!"

Bob explained to his father. "I'm sorry, Dad, we had nowhere to wash her clean. Bob's dad, Jim, got serious as he inspected the car inside and out. He walked back and forth, giving the car a thorough inspection.

Then he said, "I'm sorry, son, you must drive the car to San Francisco." Jim waited for a response.

Bill responded. "Gee, Dad, that sounds great, but why would you say that?

"Son, the war started for us here at Boeing Airplane in 1939. FDR has McDonald Douglas and us in California going flat out supplying our Allies in Europe with warplanes. We are manufacturing and delivering B-17s at breakneck speed. Our engineering team expects to start delivery of the new B-29 "Superfortress" any day now. After that, we will have to ramp up production even more. Bill Boeing believes the whole country will go to war by the end of the year. I will have no time for driving any time soon."

Bob asked. "Can we at least go get some dinner, Dad?

Jim replied. "Sure, follow me; we can head over to the cafeteria.

"The engineers eat separately from the many production workers," Jim explains to Bill and Able. "You're lucky, tonight is steak night."

Bill Boeing has prime-cut Angus beef flown in from Texas. Just load up your plates from the buffet table, then tell the chef how you want your steak cooked?" In less than 20 minutes, we were presented with New York-styled, flame-grilled to perfection rare and medium rare steaks. After dining, Jim talked about his work. The engineering group, the guys, work 7 days a week. When the pressure of constant stress builds up to a near-explosive point, Bill Boeing can give an engineer off for a couple of weeks. Bill Boeing respects all the people who work for him. Jim tells his son. "Son, When I get my break, I plan to fly into San Francisco to pick up my new car. Then I will drive to San Jose to enjoy the company of a good friend."

Bob replied enthusiastically. "You can count on me and Abel to have the car looking perfect and ready with a full tank of gas, Dad."

Jim hadn't mentioned his friend is a fun-loving female. Unfortunately, his mom no longer lives in Seattle. Bob would later learn his mom and dad are living separate lives. Jim apologized.

"I have to get back to work."

Goodbyes were said. It was time to get back on the road again.

On the road again, both agreed. What extraordinary good fortune the two were having. Bob told Abel that he was raised in a family of adventurers. "Growing up, we would prepare for an adventure. "We chose a travel destination. Acquire the right gear. Then set out to explore the world as we traveled. Right now, Abel, we are on an Adventure."

1941

The Pacific highway boasts a paved road stretching 1600 miles from the Canadian border to Mexico. Much of the road corners steeply through towering evergreen trees and follows the rocky ocean coast. Passing slow traffic presents a real challenge. Logging trucks on the road by sheer size. The big rigs go slowly up the hills carrying heavy loads. Occasionally they run downhill at breakneck speeds. Because either the brakes are hot enough to burn or, even worse, friction-hot brakes catch fire, setting the massive tires on fire and then turning the log truck into an inferno. Travel hint if you smell rancid oil or burnt metal.

Get past the smelly truck or pull over. Stay out of their way!

Spectacular coastal views abound. The road winds past impenetrable cliffs on one side of the road and a steep cliffside leading to the Pacific Ocean. The key to driving these stretches is to pass slow motorists when you find a safe straight site line, often taking 30 minutes or more. Inevitably you will share the road with more reckless drivers. Someday, these people may crash and burn. Don't let them take you with them. Hasta la vista.

Bob drives past Olympia. Noticing the Washington State Capital, Abel teases Bob. "We must have made a wrong turn back there. That looks like the National Capitol Rotunda."

Bob drives through Aberdeen to Highway 101. "This is a logging country where massive logs are rafted down the river below. Log trucks are coming and going in every direction. Soon they are traveling South hugging the Washington coast to Oregon."

Abel says, "If we go South on 101, not North, we will be in Seaside, Oregon before dark. North 101 would take us around the Olympic mountains, then back to Seattle on a slow windy road."

Bill replied. "We don't want that." Bill takes the road into the small town of Seaside, Oregon. The sunsets over the Pacific Ocean and a sign proclaiming peace.

SEASIDE OREGON
Everything BUT WAR!

IF YOU WANT TO FIGHT, GO TO:
HELL
NORWAY   4566
SHANGHAI   5,703
TOKIO   4,777
LONDON   4,782
PEIPING   5,396
PARIS   4,993
GIBRALTAR   5,462
HONG KONG   6,471
BERLIN   5,041
SIDNEY   6,886
OSLO   4,591

The national signs pointed in all directions. Abel watched Bob; he was in deep thought. He responded. "Hmm, it appears the vote is 11 to 1. We are at war. I wish Seaside, Oregon, the best of luck as peaceniks." We drove off looking for a place to camp. We purchased a small tent and raincoats before leaving Seattle. The Oregon coast gets a lot of rain, even sometimes in the summertime. We pulled into a pullover spot 12 miles out of town. We set up camp before our canvas tent turned soggy under rain-drenched clouds. The morning sunshine dried the tent well enough to throw it into the trunk. After a quick breakfast of fresh apples, we drove off in search of hot coffee and pancakes. Cannon Beach Surfside Road Cafe served us plate-size stacked pancakes and coffee for 35 cents each and a dime for the black brew.

I told Bob I'm sure I could drive fine enough. How hard could it be? Bob wasn't convinced. "I promised dad I would keep his car safe and secure." Bob would just grip the steering wheel tighter and troop on. We pulled over, camped again, enjoyed the sights, and proceeded carefully. When we entered the California National Redwood Forest, Bob was exhausted. We thought we would be in San Francisco by the end of the day. One last hard push and they would find a place to kick back, and so it seemed.

Bob said. "Today I am planning to drive slow tourist style. I am not worrying about passing anybody. I am going to poke along like tourists do and take lots of breaks. I might even stop and hug one of these big Redwood trees." Abel said nothing. He knew patience was not one of Bob's many positive traits. He, too, was getting tired. Abel would be all eyes and ears.

Redwood trees are the tallest trees on earth. Growing upwards of 300 feet. If our traveling companions were here 100 years earlier, in 1841, the view would be little changed. These trees are as old as 3500 years. They would not be recognizably taller. Bob and Abel are awestruck as they proceed through the forest. Their souls are revived, and their bodies are exhausted.

Not all the California trees are protected from ambitious timbermen. Not long after driving through the protected Redwood Forest, fleets of log trucks took possession of the road. At first, the travelers felt fresh and invigorated. Slowly tensions of the long drive resumed. Just when the road began to open, free of congestion. It appeared calamity lay ahead. Something big was tumbling down the steep hillside. An overturned log truck had lost its load of massive timbers. Instinctively Bob threw the Plymouth coupe into first gear and hit the brakes hard. Stopping in the middle of the road was not good enough. A tsunami of humongous logs barreled down the hill toward them. Bob slammed the Plymouth in reverse and then jammed the throttle to the floor. Instinctively Abel grabbed the door handle to hang on.

They were too frightened to breathe. Many forest rounds came to rest in a chaotic display, yet a final treed bruiser persisted towards them. Abel exhaled then forcefully gulped in a life-forced air. He shouted. "Get Off the Road!" Abel pointed to the refuge of a side logging road. Bob swung the car hard. His left foot was fast, stuck full throttle to the floor. As the mighty log rolled past, Bob instinctively braked to a stop on the narrow dirt side road. All the travelers wanted to do was get the hell out of the car. Fortune has it they found walking a short distance, the end of the road was an overlook to the great Pacific Ocean. Tall grey rolling waves made their way to the beach. The tall white crested waves completed their journey diminished in a thump on the claw-shaped rocks below. Each incoming tide slowly calmed the nerves of the frazzled travelers. Bob said. "We were damn lucky."

"You got that one right," replied Able, and that was it. The big event was over. Bob and Abel proceeded to San Francisco in an ordinary fashion. There are times in life when the ordinary is extraordinary. This was one of those times.

Chapter 8

Skittle Skedaddle Doo

Kate has set down roots, shallow though they may be in New York. Married. Headed for a new life out West. Now she must rip out those shallow roots to start her life again. Kate has said her goodbyes to her small community of friends and associates. A degree of respect is given a sense of value, and life for the moment is explored.

Kate took a seat on the train to San Francisco, thinking. "In one week, a new life will start again. I hope Abel is settled in well." What will work at the Revlon Counter be like?" Mostly Kate wanted to be as far away from Alphonso as possible. She hoped to never see that man again. Riding the Transcontinental West, Kate viewed a blur of passing towns, cities, and countryside connected by railroad station stops. Kate ate like a bird and mostly slept. She was there in San Francisco in no time. She departed the train. There stood Abel waiting in the train station. He called out to Kate. "Hello, gorgeous. Do you fancy going my way?"

Kate replied. "Why of course, my good man."

Being in San Francisco together felt like the first evening of marriage all over again. Kate arrived in the city refreshed and rested. Together they compared travel experiences. Abel shared with Kate the many road trip adventures they encountered. Kate could not help but think. But life with Abel would be exciting. Abel had found a cute little cottage to live in. One bedroom, a small kitchen, and a private bathroom. No embarrassing trips down the hall to a shared bathroom. Kate told Abel as they snuggled into bed. "It's perfect. It feels like our home." Tomorrow, she starts her new Revlon Cosmetics Counter sales job.

Kate woke up early. She was out of the door before 6:00 AM. Her makeup was perfect. Smiling confidently, Kate navigated the bus route to the West Coast Emporium. Kate stood in front of the store, surprised to see such a plain store. The Revlon counter may be noteworthy in size and accompaniments. Kate swung the entry door wide open and charged in. To Kate's utter amazement, nothing in the store looked familiar on a grand scale. Kate found a uniformed sales clerk and asked. "Can you direct me to the store manager? I have an open appointment as a Revlon sales representative." Kate followed the directions to the manager's office. Kate knocked on the door. Mr. Merced invited her into his office, then asked her. "What may I help you with?"

Kate replied. " I am here by appointment from the New York Selfridge Store to manage and assist sales in the Revlon Sales Department. I have with me my letters of recommendation." Mr. Merced extended his hand and then examined the paperwork, replying.

"Yes, everything appears to be in good order. Please sit down, Kate. I am afraid we have never heard of you. You have been duped. Our Revlon counter is fully staffed. No one plans to leave anytime soon." Kate, the consummate professional, lost it. She broke down and cried. Feeling sorry for Kate, Mr. Merced offered her a floor sales job. Kate left the store, accepting the sales clerk position. It was a start. She would bring home a pay check. Unfortunately, the promised work Alphonso offered her never materialized. Kate pledged to forget that terrible Alphonso ever existed. Kate even smiled, content to go to her new cottage home.

The following day, Kate was made an official employee with a new uniform. Kate was fitted below the kneecap with an olive-colored pleated skirt and topped with a cream-colored blouse. Gone were the New York high fashions from Selfridge. No matter to Kate. She had a respectable husband to keep her feeling content.

Working in a retail store kept Kate on her toes. She learned the store inventory, helped customers shop, and restocked sold items from the shelf. 2 weeks later, Kate learned how much smaller her pay checks are compared to New York. The cost of living in San Francisco is much smaller, with a population of just 300,000 compared to New York City's 13,000,000.

When Kate asked Abel why they were living in such a remote location? Abel got excited and spoke. "Honey, the great cities like Paris, London, Tokyo, and New York City are already bursting at the seams. The entire West Coast of California is ready to explode with growth. When it does, I want to own a great piece of it. We can own this view acreage location at a bargain price." Until that growth happens, they must walk a mile to catch a bus and have only one neighbor.

At the end of June, Kate told Able. "It has been 2 months since my menstrual flow. I am certain that I am pregnant. I can feel my body changing."

Abel replied. "That's great, Isn't it?"

"Yes, honey it is." Kate responded. "We need to discuss my work and childcare plans when we have a child at home."

Abel said. "We have enough money from the shipping business to get by. Most important is to keep you and our future baby boy happy."

Kate told Able. "It could be a girl, you know."

"I imagine so." Replied Able.

Returning to work pregnant got Kate thinking. "It has been nice to have work. However, there is talk of an eminent retail workers' strike." Kate plans to jump ship and try something new. This Saturday, welder candidates are encouraged to try out welding for hire at Kaiser shipbuilding. Starting pay is triple what Kate makes for retail work. Kate finds her mood is buoyed at work. The other employees have no idea what has Kate acting so happy.

Old man Kaiser knows America is going to War, and when they do, many of his men welders will leave the country to fight overseas. They won't be drafting women. When the Great War begins, he will need women welders and lots of them. Lucky for them, they will get equal pay and better consideration. William Kaiser wants to be the first

to hire many women welders. This Saturday, he will
give the ladies a trial chance to see if they have the
talent to be great welders. William Kaiser needs to
fill his new Richmond Shipyard with many more
workers.

Kate traveled to the waterfront warehouse listed as
the contest hiring site. Many blue sparks flew inside
the tin structure. Outside, a giant sign advertised:

> Welders Wanted.
> Great Pay.
> Flexible Hours.
> Support our Troops now.

A large group of women of all ethnicities queued
outside. Kate joined the line. Mostly the women
chattered in anticipation of the opportunity to make
a fair wage and be part of something completely
new. Kate got caught up in the excitement. The
long wait to show talent seemed like just minutes.

It was her turn to shine. Kate was ready. First, Kate
was instructed to wear the safety eye and face
protection mask, and then she was given thick
welder gloves to protect her hands. Safety outfitted
in welder's gear, Kate could scarcely see, and her
hands felt fat and clumsy. The welding Instructor
and Inspector, Aiden, told Kate, "Watch what I do. I
am going to perform 4 separate types of welds.

Watch very carefully. Next, I want you to try and demonstrate each of the four welds. Try not to get too frustrated. Just try to do your best." Kate is fascinated with the new world of welding. She can't wait to make the blue sparks fly and fuse the clamped metals together. First, Kate welded two horizontal pieces of metal, making neat even metal pools from left to right. Satisfied with her neat and tidy welds, Kate commented. "Like pipe frosting on a cake."

Aiden said. "That is a very good-looking weld, now see if you can't make it as nice vertical and diagonal. Kate slowly and methodically completed the next 2 welds. "Simply amazing." Replied Aiden. He said, "Kate, the last weld is tricky. Try your best. Calling the weld tricky made Kate nervous and apprehensive. She wanted to do a good job, but now she was shaking. Kate told herself she had been Abel to deal with self-doubt by being focused and persevering. Kate slowly and methodically began the most difficult weld, The overhead weld. Kate stared up at a weld with hot molten metal ready to shower down on her. Kate also needed to spatially adjust to this unnatural work area. Kate does not realize that many of today's trial welders will be offered employment simply for showing elementary skills. Finally, Kate finished the overhead weld. It was not perfect. Kate turned to

the Inspector and sadly murmured. "I'm so very
sorry it is not very good."

Aiden hollered out to his boss, Frank. "Come take a
look at this." Frank came over and inspected Kate's
welds, then he said. "You are not trying to
BULLSHIT me, are you?" Aiden spoke to Kate.
"You have done some very impressive welding for
us here today. I want you to relax, take a deep
breath and show Frank you are a confident welder.
Now Kate could proceed with confidence. Aiden
liked her work. Frank watched as Kate performed
the first 3 welds precisely.

Frank said. "Those are very good Kate. Now let's
see how you do with the challenging overhead
welding." Kate focused, got in position, then started
welding. She lifted her mask to inspect her work
when she completed the weld. It was not perfect. It
could have been better.

Frank got excited. He turned to Aiden and said.
"Not bad. Do you think Uncle Sam's inspectors
would pass off on it?"

Aiden replied. "Indeed, I do."

Frank rubbed his hands together and told Aiden. "I
suggest you get her up to the office and make her
an offer. Then get the paperwork filled out."

Walking up to the office, Aiden explained to Kate that she was the first novice to perform welding at that level of proficiency. He proposed they could start her on an accelerated apprenticeship. Kate will be a journeyman welder expedited at full Journeyman pay as soon as she is up to speed.

Chapter 9

At War

The mundane task of getting on a bus, then transferring to another bus, and finally walking the mile up to the villa cottage seemed quick and effortless. It was not. Kate's mind is full of enthused expectations. Who would have thought Kate would be working in a traditional man's job at the heart of industrial shipbuilding. Doing manly work. Making top dollar pay. She considered moving to America a brilliant move for both her and Able.

Kate's buoyant move was immediately deflated as she entered her home. Abel sat slumped At his desk. A cut crystal glass rested in his right hand. The bourbon glass is half empty. A bottle of Kentucky fine bourbon rested next to the glass. Abel seldom drank. When he did partake, it was for festive or lamentable occasions. Obviously, Abel is

not in a celebratory mood. Kate said. "Hello, Able."
She waited for him to speak.

Abel looked up and told his wife. He had been
looking out the window for who knows how long.
Perhaps Abel was waiting for the booze to soften
the pain. He spoke to Kate in a clear, quiet tone. A
single tear traveled down his cheek." The King
David has been sunk. All hands have been lost.
Our flagship came to rest in shallow waters,
partially blocking the entrance and exit of the Suez
Canal. The bow gunner crew was able to get
counter shots off before the first missile hit. The
surfaced German attack submarine first struck our
ship in the bow by a torpedo. The sub then was
able to get off 2 more lethal torpedoes that hit the
King David broadside, obliterating the ship. Our
ship went down in an explosive fireball, and all
hands were lost. Our British shoreline protective
batteries finished off the vulnerable German
submarine. Tore the damn thing to pieces. So now
it, too, must be salvaged from shallow waters to
free the Canal for business. To make matters
worse, espionage is expected. Our ship previously
left under cover of darkness on a dark moonless
night. The King David should have enjoyed a clear
passage. I must tell you that damn German sub
was on a suicide mission flanked by modern
weaponry." Abel looked at Kate. He had a fire in his

eyes when he spoke with a venomous tongue. "How did they know when we were leaving the harbor? There must be a traitor lurking in Cairo. It is up to others to sort it all out. What can I do when I am living so far away?"

Kate knew Abel wasn't expecting an answer from her. He was just blowing off steam. Abel had every right to be sad and angry. By morning, Abel is back to looking for solutions to problems. Abel apologizes for being a moody bastard.

At last, Kate can share her exciting prospects to become a journeyman ship welder with Abel. Kate proposed a celebration. "Why don't we invite Bob over for BBQ steaks?"

Abel replied. "Yeah, maybe he can bring some good French Bordeaux wine that he can get past our rationing and the French zone interdict." (The Forbidden Zone.)

Bob brought an ample supply of Rothschild Chateau LaTour red wine, the good stuff. Why not? Not every day in 1941 is a lady accepted into an ironworkers' apprenticeship. What the hell? Bob is always ready to drink good wine and celebrate friendship. Yesterday, Abel mopped about complaining about losing his flagship King David. Today Abel is Mr. Carpe Diem. After talking to Bob, he is ready to purchase a new, faster, larger ship built on the East Coast of America. He just needs to work out the details to choose his next flagship. After 2 bottles of wine are emptied, Able's tongue begins to wag. "Let me tell you a thing or two about Egypt."

Kate and Bob, slightly buzzed, are content to listen to Abel. He began. "My being a Cambridge graduate, I know a thing or two about the British campaign in Africa. It was the French, whose blessed wine we enjoy today, that campaigned to construct the Suez Canal. They did this in the mid-1800s. With the help of the host country Egypt. Ten years later, the working canal was open for business. The English were total stinkers during the construction. They gave no financial support to the Egyptians. They went so far as to organise a boycott of investors to sabotage their financing. The first year of operation, it was 75% British ships that passed through the Canal. Confronted with a massive 4-million-dollar debt and high operating cost, the Egyptian Ismail sold the Canal to British Prime Minister Benjamin Disraeli. The British purchased exclusive control of the Canal. They safeguard the financial and security of the Canal. They held off a Turkish invasion in 1918 WWI and I believe they will have successful dominion in this War as well. Despite the fact they didn't properly safeguard my flagship. They should maintain the sovereignty of the Suez Canal. God help us all if they don't." Abel poured himself a final half glass of Bordeaux. He then found some peace. He parked his tongue in the side of his mouth and politely listened.

President Franklin Delano Roosevelt addressed Congress to request a Declaration of War. His famous speech was broadcasted live around much of the world. The opening remarks stated.

> *YESTERDAY, December 7, 1941,*
> *a date which will live in infamy, the*
> *United States of America was*
> *suddenly and deliberately attacked*
> *by the Naval and Air Forces of the*
> *Empire of Japan.*

Abel had been briefed yesterday by Adonis from the Cairo Shellhorn Shipping Office of the attack on America. It was hard to comprehend then as it is now being heard a day later live on the radio. Abel turned to his wife and then said. "I was certain this War was inevitable, yet I somehow feel shocked at the immensity of being at war with the world."

Kate replied. "I cannot imagine how all this will affect us." Then Kate quietly thought I ran from the bombing of London. This time, for this War, there is no place else I want to run to. This is my new home, and I will fight to keep it. Kate is glad she is laboring to support the American war effort.

Garret Shellhorn Shipping

Garret Shellhorn knew he could live many lifetimes and never find the fabulous Star of Africa Diamond again. His prize must be held secure until he secured the gemstone in a vault in Switzerland. So Garret Shellhorn set out to find and purchase a boat that could be seaworthy and fend off pirates. He found an 80-foot wood-planked Viking ship plated in iron which he fashioned with modern armaments, then added a hidden security safe. The vessel is powered by steam or sail and was purchased from a Norwegian shipyard. Garrett commissioned a trusted companion and captain of the sea, El Greco. Garret telegram requested his partnership in the launching of the Shellhorn Shipping Company. El Greco accepted the partnership offer by telegram. Many letters and advancement of funds followed.

A year and one half later, Garret's Star of Africa Diamond was removed from hiding and secreted aboard the Vaerdalen Viking Ship, Garrett's new Norwegian-built cargo ship. Garrett boarded the ship employing the sea mastery of Captain El Greco. The Vaerdalen proved the perfect vessel to clandestine gold and diamonds along the pirated Coast of Africa.

In later years Garrett learned he needed a larger and faster ship to move cargo throughout the Mediterranean Sea and into Atlantic ports. The German Shipbuilders of Bremen built the most competitive vessels at the time. The newly commissioned ship exceeded 900 feet in length and traveled an incredible 27 knots. Garrett Shellhorn knew he was taking a tremendous risk buying the finest passenger and cargo ship in the world. Instantly, Garrett owned prestige and clout in the international shipping business. He christened his ship King David. Three years and two months to the ship's inaugural cruise day. She was sunk in the shallow waters exiting the Suez Canal. All hands lost. When Garrett Shellhorn was asked. "Do you regret purchasing The King David?"

He replied. "Absolutely not. The crew and passengers all knew the risk. But, of course, I feel bad for the loss of life and property. Insurance payment allowed me to finance the construction of The King David II, and she is still going strong. My Entire financial foundation has always remained solvent from my profits in mining diamonds and gold. "The business of life must go on."

Chapter 10

Cabin boy

Adonis is the proud son of his mother, Cassandra. The name Adonis implies handsome. Adonis is a rather plain tall skinny lad growing up in Greece. His father is a fisherman that has taught his son the ways of the sea. His mother entertains hope of her son becoming a great man of the sea. To do this, he must harness the teachings of his humble but poor fishermen's livelihood. Secretly she reaches out to a man she once knew intimately. She telegrammed Garrett Shellhorn in South Africa.

Dear Garret, my son needs a better future. Please find it in your heart to employ him in your shipping company. Cassandra.

The mother and son waited for a reply. Every day Adonis would ask. "Momma, is there any news? Eventually, Garrett responded with good news. Adonis could begin his new apprenticeship if they could get their son to the Shellhorn, Cairo Shipping office. Money is saved, and provisions are stored in Apollo's small fishing boat. This is Adonis' first long trip in a boat. Eventually, the father and son arrive in Cairo, where they find the Shellhorn shipping dock. Adonis bids farewell to his father with a new appreciation for his father's skill at sea.

Adonis introduced himself to the Shipping office staff. Inquiries revealed it would be at least a week before the South African "Vaerdalen" arrives in Port. Then it will be at least 2 days before returning to South Africa. While at the office, Adonis learns the Scandinavian-built ship is 83 feet long, beam 16 feet, and depth of 5' 1", built of timbered wood and iron steel skinned hull. She is a twin mast sailing schooner with an auxiliary 84-horse-powered coal-fired steam single screw propeller.

Adonis is a skinny lad. He was taught by his parents not to steal. Adonis remembers. "The first day, I had no money and no food. On the second day I carefully pinched a crumb or two to eat. So, I was not going to starve; I made certain that I did not get caught pinching food."

Joyously, Adonis welcomes the sight of the Vaerdalen docking. First to disembark is Garrett Shellhorn; he is eager to size up this Greek boy. His inspection reveals. The boy certainly needs some fattening up. I would hate to see a gust of wind send him overboard. I do see where he looks like his mother. Thank goodness I see nothing in his face that looks like me. Adonis waited for Garrett's break in concentration. Then said, "Permission to come aboard sir."

"Why yes, do come aboard," welcomed Garrett.

In the dark night, Garrett crept into the captain's quarters and opened the hidden safe to remove the secured diamonds. Garrett then transferred the valuable diamonds to the office safe, where they would be shipped to Rome, Paris, and London to be refined into finely cut gems. To reduce the threat of theft, all transfers have been made singularly by a well-armed single merchant of Shellhorn Shipping. The motto is safe, not sorry.

The following day, Adonis, the cabin boy, boarded Vaerdalen with the captain El Greco Viejo, the "Old Greek," the name given to him by Garrett Shellhorn. He and the ship's crew set sail for South Africa. The vessel is loaded with cargo to barter along the coast of Africa. They would later arrive at home Port with new wealth and supplies for Garret Shellhorn's personal mining needs. Adonis could have no idea that in 5 years, he would be made captain of the Vaerdalen. A lot can happen in 5 years.

El Greco spoke. "Today is December 7th, you have worked with us for one year. You will have a special visitor today." El Greco was never one to waste words. El Greco with a head full of wild thick white hair, a wind and sun wrinkled face. Always commandeering a pipe clenched in yellow tobacco-stained teeth. Yet, despite his weathered appearance, he is really a good skipper. The year is 1929.

December 7th, 1929.

Garrett steps aboard Vaerdalen. He and Adonis are alone on the ship. Garrett closely examines the lad and then says. "Shaving off the thin whiskers growing under your nose would serve you well. It makes you look too young. 17 Years ago, I knew your mother well. Your mother is a good woman. The both of us would like to see you do well. All I have to say is watch and learn, then you will have a bright future with us." Garrett left the ship. That was all that was said.

The following day before the captain and crew returned to the ship. Adonis had his first shave with a sharp shell. After that, Adonis purchased a straight edge when his facial hair thickened, useful for shaving and self-protection. During his first year aboard the ship, Adonis took to seafaring like a duck to water. His payment for work is a full belly, a spirited crew to chat with, and the value of doing an honest day's work.

Age 16

The cabin boy is really a young man. At Garrett Shellhorn's insistence, a newly paid merchant seaman. Earning Up to $1.25 a day depending on available ship-to-shore work. Adonis is promoted to deckhand and is the primary breadwinner for his home family in Greece.

At the age of 18, Adonis has the distinction of being the second longest-serving crew member aboard the Vaerdalen captained by El Greco. He has the rank of bosun, in charge of the deck crew. His wage increased to $1.75 a day. Pay is earned for days of loading and unloading of cargo. There is a new opportunity to participate in paid work, doubling his monthly pay. Mom and Dad are incredibly grateful for the income sent home. The small Greek fishing village recognizes Adonis's family status and charitable giving. The 1931 depression struck Greece hard; starving families searched the world for better conditions. The Adonis family home stood out amongst the village houses. Their family home is freshly painted and greets a passer-by with colorful planter boxes displaying bright red geraniums.

At 21, newly captained Adonis takes charge of the Vaerdalen. El Greco was promoted to head the Cairo Shellhorn Shipping Office. The ambitious Adonis immediately makes changes. The first order of business Adonis took to task was to prepare the ship and men to fight off an attack if needed. He trained the men in the proficiency of small arms fire. Weapons are retrieved quickly and fired accurately on targets. Adonis installed an automatic rapid-firing gun hidden in the stern well. A crew member is added to watch and shoot all hostiles. Safeguards and training in place. The cargo is upgraded to enhance profitability. Gone are the days of transporting bananas and cooking fuel. The cargo hull is full. Valuable barrels of diesel fuel, coal, and building timbers. The dock workers notice the profitable cargo upgrade from the Vaerdalen deck. Word gets out to pirates. It is time to do a little investigating.

Adonis grew up fishing with his father on the Mediterranean Sea; they, too, had pirates. Adonis could smell a pirate a mile off. Adonis spied the approaching fast boat; he asked his stern gunner. "What do you think of the boat headed our way? I think she may be full of pirates, Sir."

Adonis hollered to his crew. "All Hands Prepare For Hostilities." This was not a drill. Feet scrambled, guns are fully loaded and aimed at the fast-approaching vessel. The gunner yelled, "Thirty seconds to impact." No order needed to be given; it was an imminent threat. All weapons are discharged on target. Adonis and the crew looked in dismay. Bits of blood-soaked timbers dotted the water. No sign of visible life. It is best to leave the debris quickly, no questions asked.

The word got out up and down the coast. "Don't fuck with the crew of the Vaerdalen, It ain't worth it." The Vaerdalen, under the stewardship of Adonis and crew, often was more profitable than far larger ships working up and down the African coast. Many years later, the old worn, and outdated Vaerdalen was retired. The vessel and crew added to the coffer's vast wealth by transporting valuable diamonds. Only the chosen knew of the rich bounty hidden below deck in the many years of service.

Garrett took great pleasure in traveling twice a year with Adonis to Cairo, Egypt, to secure his business ties. So, when it came time to install a new Cairo Shellhorn Shipping Officer, there was only one choice. Adonis. Adonis' record is flawless. In years of service, not a single diamond is unaccounted for. Never a pirate boarding. Always a highly skilled crew and a productive purchase and sale of cargo.

Garret Shellhorn officiated the Cairo Memorial service for El Greco for members of Shellhorn Shipping. An abundance of food and beverage was served and enjoyed. We drank and ate heartily. Our lives have no surpluses during the austerity of the 1930s. In a hushed conversation, we inquired about the Christian name of El Greco. No one seemed to have an answer. For sure, the Old Dutch Man knew. He planned to ship the body back to Greece for a family funeral. El Greco travels home first class aboard the Mediterranean Lord Stanley Flagship in a cast iron Fisk metallic burial case. That thing must weigh a ton. Garret Shellhorn pinches every penny and then goes out for a send-off to the dead.

Adonis, dressed in a fine wool outfit, feels the hot African sun. Sweat trickles down the nape of his neck. He sticks with the crew of the Vaerdalen. The crew are all present and accounted for. Adonis impatiently waits for his private meeting that Garret has mandated aboard his ship. Adonis wonders if they will meet aboard the newer, larger Lord Stanley or the Vaerdalen.

Garrett said. "That's all folks, you can get back to your own lives. That is good food and booze, it cost me a pretty penny. Clean it up and take it all home." We obliged. Garret called out to Adonis. "I am going to the dock, meet me at your ship." That was the first time he ever referred to the Vaerdalen as my ship.

Adonis remembers following Garrett into the captain's quarters. I followed him in. He ordered me to lock the door. Then he removed a panel revealing a formidable safe. "Watch me and remember the combination of the safe. He told me. "Now you give it a try." Fortunately, the safe door opened after I dialled the secret numbers. Then he explained to me what the real payload cargo was. All these years, I thought we just hauled things to buy and sell along the coast of Africa, Building materials, machine parts, cooking wood, and barrels of fuel. Garrett informed me. "This 83-foot, steel-hulled Viking ship is really a clandestine treasure ship. Secreting gold and diamonds to the Mediterranean Sea. The African coast has far too many pirates playing their mischief. A humble boat such as this lures a few nasty pirates." Then Garrett dug under the benches to show and tell. "These are the latest in armaments as needed. Now you take a captain like El Greco. He knew what to do." Garret was excited and babbled. "Once, a pirate boat charged him and his crew. El Greco grabbed the wheel; he timed it perfectly. The Vaerdalen swung 180 degrees and pulverized their boat into floating fragments of timber. I pay well for risky business, that is, if you still want this job." I shook the old man's hand and then thanked him profusely.

Deja vu, I already knew what Garret was going to ask. "Are you ready to run the Cairo Shipping Office?" Garrett Shellhorn has always offered me competitive pay and ample opportunity. I did my part to make us both gain our profits. Every man has his worth. I made it my business to prosper. Both Garret and I needed the climb to the top. We sat down together to map out a partnership. I agreed with the Old Dutchman. Keep the new captain of the Vaerdalen focused on transporting worldly cargo. The fewer people that knew about the diamonds, the better.

Chapter 11

Allen

It is 32 days after conception, and Kate doesn't want to consider having a baby. Today Kate goes to work on the first day of her welding journeyman apprenticeship. Entering the Richmond Kaiser Shipyard, she is struck by the immensity of the job site. Kate stops workers darting here and there to ask for her job site location. Eventually, she enters the correct building and selects the reception table that directs Kate where to begin her new profession. An atmosphere of competition and cooperation prevails. Kate is pleased to learn she can exhibit welding proficiency much better than many new learners. The day goes by quickly, and She is learning safety procedures and welding techniques.

Today is a welding overview. First, safety gear and equipment are explained and then demonstrated.

Next, the tack weld is presented. The tack weld cements the steel material by fusing beads of metal sufficient to hold the metal securely. Finally, steel sheets are combined to form a water-impervious solid bond after a morning of safety standards and welding demonstrations. The afternoon is individual hands-on welding in front of an instructor.

Kate works with a small, easy-to-handle piece of metal. Her first assignment is to attempt to neatly tack weld 2 pieces of metal together. Once Kate and her fellow students succeed in this task, they advance their welding to fuse the two pieces of metal into a seamless, watertight solid bond. Over the following days and weeks, the apprentice welders will learn to implement these techniques onto massive thick steel sheets. They have much to learn before building the hulls of ships. Students will come and go; only the proficient welders will earn a wage in the Kaiser Richmond Shipyard.

Kate and the other graduates of the welding apprenticeship go to work paid to assemble the massive hulls of Liberty ships, 441 feet long and 57 feet wide. Based on Kate's initial success from her first try-out, welding supervisors will look for promotional candidates to do the more challenging work. All workers will be given an opportunity to advance. Kaiser is an equal-opportunity Company.

For October, there is no hiding Kate's 7th month of pregnancy. Even bulky clothes and self-jokes about getting fat didn't fool anyone of her condition. Mid-October, the Kaiser management team and her co-workers sent Kate home for maternity leave. They did first throw her a proper farewell party. More than one of the male workers gifted Kate boxes of scarce chocolates. Some of the gals sent her home with cut flowers. Kate is assured a welcome return. Now she is ready to have her baby and become a mother.

On the 27th day of December, baby Allen traveled down the birth canal into a Franciscan midwife's hands, then into his mother's loving embrace. Allen was born with the gift of a photographic memory. This is no guarantee of being of genius status. Allen is just as capable of remembering falsehoods as well as truths. Allen goes so far as to claim that he remembers his own birth. I doubt this is true. Allen has achieved many academic accomplishments and eventually becomes an African Shellhorn Shipping tycoon.

By the time Allen was born, the cottage had a new wing built, adding his nursery room and an expanded office for Able's shipping business. The Shellhorn home also welcomed Betty Davis, their new next-door cottage neighbor.

Betty proved to be the perfect addition to this rural outpost. Someone to borrow and trade kitchen supplies with. A social charm and the ideal nanny for young Allen. When the time came for Kate to return to Kaisers Shipyard. Kate had no guilt about leaving Allen behind. She was helping her country at war, and Allen was in good hands. Abel retreated to his new shipping office. Allen went next door to Betty's for care and comfort.

Allen remembers it differently. Allen remembers being at Betty's house crying for his mother. Calling for his mother's warm, soft breast milk. Having a tantrum, tossing aside the wretched watered-down evaporated milk bottle that Betty offered. The worst of it all, his mother's own milk dried up. Nothing came forth from her nippled spigots.

Allen reflected. To be fair, Betty was adequate. My childhood would have been a total shambles had it not been for Mom and Dad's reading story time. In the evening, I was often put to bed while entirely awake. What was I to do but lay there staring at the ceiling? Most certainly, the finest thing my parents did for me was teach me to read. To this day, when I want to Know something, I research it from a book. Which leads me to read more books. I do love books.

When World WarII ended, people everywhere flooded the streets to celebrate. Unfortunately, poor Betty's son Andrew never did come home. Lost at war, presumed dead. Betty had nothing to celebrate. The observant Allen entered his happy family home and exclaimed. "I don't know what people are so happy about. There will be another war." Many wars would be fought from Korea to Laos, Cambodia, and Vietnam, then from Iraq to Afghanistan. Fortunately, we have yet to see another world war anytime soon.

Abel and Kate are thrilled. Allen's book smarts and worldly observation translate into excellent competitive grades. Allen is fond of saying. "The key to achievement in school is. Learn the testing material, then tell the teacher what the teacher wants to hear." Once, Allen took issue with an instructor. He fashioned a counterargument, then presented his argument. The teacher marked Allen down to a grade B. The instructor claimed. "Your examination of the material, though worthy, was not what I sought. Allen boasted. It was the most illustrative course that I took in High School. I will never forget to consider the judge's judgment first and foremost. Allen finished high school at 16, valedictorian of his senior class. Abel talked to the

instructor that had given his son Allen a grade of B.
It wasn't hard to convince his son's instructor that
he obviously had made a mistake. The B grade
was changed to an A grade. A perfect match of As.
Even valedictorians need family support.

Of course, Allen's university could only be one
choice: London's' Cambridge. His application to
study required no additional consideration unlike
Abel had needed. So, 16-Year-old Allen is
accepted as one of the younger scholars to attend
school in London's' prestigious campus.
Cambridge University welcomes Valedictorians.
The year is 1962. Time reveals that Allen has a
bright future ahead.

Chapter 12

Shipping Out

Abel is feeling guilty. A great war is going on, and he is doing little to help win it. Instead, he is profiting from war. His ships are sunk, and men die perishing in the war-ravaged waters. At the same time, he sits in sunny California, drinking fine tea and liquoring up to hide his shame. Shame for profiting while others are fighting for freedom. He was raised to be a better man than that. Abel Shellhorn descends from a line of fierce fighting men. Dammit, he must fight.

Abel leaves home and then walks a mile to the nearest bus stop. An hour later, he is outside his best friend's home, Bob. Abel knocks on the door of the house of Bob Hansen. Bob answers the door, seeing his friend Abel looking a little forlorn. Abel asks Bob. Fancy going to get a pint? Bob is busy organizing the Democratic Party. Seeing the desperation on Able's face, Bob relinquishes his work. Then said, "sure. Where would you like to go? Let's go to the Shoremen's Pub down at the Wharf." Replied Able. Bob said. "Give me a moment to wrap things up here."

Several minutes later, Abel and Bob are sitting at the
Shoremen's Pub, already on their second glass of beer.
The Shoremen's Pub is a popular waterfront bar serving
cheap whiskey and beer to sailors. Abel and Bob wear
wool slack and linen shirts. They stand out from the
many sailors uniformed in dungarees. Abel and Bob
listen as two tables over, a man is talking. Look over at
that table of fat cats drinking. Here they are drinking in a
working man's bar. They look like they own the damn
place. If they think we will put up with their kind, they
are wrong. The talking men stood up and stared at Abel
and Bob with crazed anger. The two talkers sized up
Abel and Bob and hesitated momentarily. The shorter of
the 2 men said. "Come on Jake, let's get the hell out of
here." Stink was in the air. Bob and Abel stood up, tense
and ready to fight. As the talkers left the bar, Bob
returned with 2 shots of cheap whiskey. Abel gestured
and then said. "Bottoms up." The whiskey glasses were
empty and then slammed to the table. Bob says. "Let's
Go." Abel and Bob are pumped up and ready to fight.
As they exit the Shoremen's Pub, they look for trouble.
None is to be found.
Abel and Bob boarded the American Kate. Two oceans
and 2 years of service lay ahead. Bob is the new
American Kate Liberty ship owner, which he secreted at
a favorable price. The ship is entirely financed by
Shellhorn Shipping. All Abel must do is survive the next
2 years of war and become an American citizen. Then
claim the ship as his own. Abel is confident he will own
this American ship in 1945. By then, he has 5 years of
American residency. The only thing that can stop his
plans is death. Abel has no intention of dying any time
soon.

Two years of dangerous merchant service to his new country can't hurt. Bob and Abel will be paid double what a navy man is paid doing the same pay for doing the same work. The catch is they are far more likely to die as merchant marine sailors. You might ask why? Liberty ships travel a slow 11 knots, with little firepower making them easy targets.

To make matters worse, the enemy places a very high value on sinking these Liberty ships. Because Merchant ships supply the war with artillery with food rations, bullets, shells, and bombs, they even supply fresh troops to the frontlines. In the first year of WWII, half of the merchant ships were sunk going to the waterfront then another half were sunk upon return for new supplies. In 1942 fewer merchant ships were sunk aided by Navel-escorted artillery Ships. The Navy was assigned the role of merchant marine protection.

Bob and Abel believe being aboard the American Kate is the best of luck. The ship itself was christened the American Kate after Able's wife won the honor in a Kaiser Shipping Contest; Bob and Abel secured the very best security escort the Navy had to offer; a favor granted by FDR himself. Their Captain Blanque is an outstanding skipper. The time for adventure and glory is at hand. What could possibly go wrong?

The Kaiser Shipyard Has Done It!
Our Richmond San Francisco Bay Kaiser Shipbuilding yard has built an entire war-ready ocean-going ship in one week.

Kaiser now has 10 days to ensure the damn thing floats and continues to float well. The ship will be christened the American Kate, named after top contest welder Kate

Shellhorn. Kaiser's engineers and quality control inspectors cover every inch of the vessel, ensuring the integrity of assembly and construction. The Kaiser Ship's reputation is at stake.

The press corps and a throng of dignitaries are assembled at the ship's giant launch rails. Abel and Bob see Kate looking tiny, far below. Kate's Champagne bottle is held firmly in both hands. Whack, the bottle explodes in a crescendo of bubbles. Tons upon tons of steeled ship thunder down the rails. She Floats! Rolling, then swaying back and forth, simultaneously bobbing up and down. The crowd thunders applause. Amplified dignitaries struggle to be heard amongst the roar of the public. Success. The American Kate is launched and ready for war.

It takes a month plus to build a Liberty ship from start to finish for the Richmond Kaiser Shipyard located on the San Francisco Bay east of San Francisco. So let's show the world we can build a Liberty Ship in a week. To make this publicity stunt work, they would secretly assemble the ship first in giant components. Then, call in the press and engage the best production crews to work around the clock. As an added incentive naming rights to the new ship would go to the top welder.

Kate loves to compete for a coveted prize. The Shellhorn family invites Betty over to get in on the fun. Kate shares with Betty and her family how important winning this competition is. Kate declares she needs a combined effort to win. She plans to eat, breathe, and weld for the next week of the competition. That means you, my family, and my friends will oversee the home front. "Understood?"

Ready Set Go

102 Naval and Merchant Marines make up the crew of the newly constructed American Kate personnel readying the ship for its inaugural cruise. The ship is commanded by Captain Donald Blanque and his First Officer Lorenzo DePaul, who served as First Officer of the crew. The American Kate set sail across the San Francisco Bay with a skeleton crew of a dozen sailors en route to the Oakland Bay Terminus. The bay crossing should take less than 2 hours from dock to dock. Captain Blanque has sufficiently staffed the ship to meet its immediate needs for engineers in the engine room, a helmsman for piloting from the bridge, and a deck crew to safely secure the American Kate to the docking and loading facilities in Oakland.

Immediately upon docking, personnel hiring and loading commence. A war is going on, and there is no time to waste. A team of civilian longshoremen begins loading the ship. This is a maiden voyage. Supplies are stored to run food services.

Plates, cups, bowls, and flatware are needed. Salt, pepper, spices, and sugar must be stored. Food… Fresh and frozen meat, large tins of food items, Potatoes, rice, and pasta. Maybe even smoked cured hams for special occasions. The local dock workers are employed 24 hours a day for the next few weeks.

Elsewhere on the ship, tools and maintenance supplies get stored in the engine room. Above decks, replacement ropes and safety and rescue gear are stored, protected from the harsh sea elements. Sleeping quarters are fitted with new pillows and blankets.

A naval team is assigned to the ship. This group of 23 Navy men is reading the ship to fight off an air or sea attack. The ship is armed with 50-caliber rapid gunfire and 5-millimeter rocket shells. Depth charges are stowed away for blowing up German submarines known to even hunt along the California coast. The Navy sailors are commissioned by the Navy to secure the Merchant Marine ship. Queries.

70 New merchant marine sailors are hired as deckhands and crewmates. They are not conscripted. Once back in Port, they can return home by choice. Abel and Bob are assigned to this deck crew responsible for loading and unloading the American Kate. They are also expected to aid in the ship's defense at sea as needed. They will also assist in cleaning and maintenance of the vessel. Of course, Captain Blanque has absolute authority over each and every crewmember and Navy personnel.

The Skipper, Don Blanque, has double-checked with his first officer Larenzo DePaul and his 5 key officers that the ship is properly ready and equipped to set sail. Their crew of 102 personnel is fit and capable of serving. There is no looking back as they pull away from the Oakland dock. The call to the engine room for 84 RPM, 11 knots headway, is given. 2500 Steam horsepower drives one enormous propeller moving nearly 500 feet of ship out to the Pacific Ocean. The Captain and crew set a heading for the South Pacific. When they are near Japan, they will be in the thick of it. Hostile waters lay far ahead. Today they feel at ease as they join a large convoy of merchant ships headed to the South Pacific Theater. Secured by Naval aircraft carriers and destroyers of heavy-armed battalion ships. If need be, this ship can travel an astounding 17,000 nautical miles before refueling. Technically the ship could travel to the South Pacific to return to San Francisco, then back to the South Pacific again. No Captain would ever run a ship's fuel down to empty. Even during the war, a crew requires legs put to solid earth after perilous travels. A blast of the mighty horn deafens Able's ears signaling the ship's departure; he jumps in response, and Bob says to Able. "Will you look at that? There are warships as far as the eyes can see. Abel responded. Yes, it makes me feel safe." A navy gunner was listening called out. "Just wait for when we enter the South Pacific." Bob and Abel had nothing to worry about now. They just kicked back and enjoyed the inaugural cruise. That Navy gunner had seen action before. He had been in the combat zone. His name is Sergeant Warnisky. He liked to spit out the end piece of a new cigar and then exclaim in a booming voice. "Just call me Sergeant War. Then he would puff and spit and carry on. He is not the highest-ranking Navy man aboard. Still, he is the most popular of the enlisted men serving on the American Kate.

Chapter 13

Fuego

Bob and Abel entered the small quarters of their shared cabin. The cabin consisted of a bunk bed unit with a storage unit under the bed. A small desk with a built-in lower storage unit is at the end of the room. Bob asked Able. "Is it ok if I take the lower bunk?"

"Yeah sure." replied Able.

Before Bob stowed his belongings, he carefully took out the drawer unit. He looked intently at the drawer and its capacity. Finally, he appeared to be satisfied. Bob announced to Abel with enthused vigor. "This should be a good cruise." Abel didn't know what to say. All he could think. We are going to the South Pacific, where the Japanese would likely have angry gunners shooting at the ship. We are at war! Abel decided to not pay any attention to Bob. He needed to just let things work themselves out. After Bob and Abel stowed their few possessions, they agreed to go to the deck and look about.

Bob and Abel found a seat on the deck. It is exciting to be part of such a big seafaring convoy. The air is permeated with heavy bunker fuel exhausted from the many ships. Breazy wind conditions send salted mist to the deck from the wakes of the Navy battalion group ahead. The American Kate has left the San Francisco Bay to rendezvous with the Navy escort and the protected fleet of Merchant Ships. Abel tells Bob. "I think we should enjoy feeling secure for now, don't you think?" Bob grinned and then said. "Right oh!"

1730, {5:30 PM}

Mess call announcement. Bob said, Let's go get something to eat. Abel responds. "Yeah, I'm hungry as hell." The galley crew is serving its first meal. They have opened numerous tins of beef stew, heated them hot, then served bread and butter for supper. For dessert, cans of peaches are dispensed into serving bowls. The ship maintains a constant supply of coffee and desalination water to drink and cook with. Even the ship's decks are sprayed free of corrosive salt water. Cleaning bow to stern with desalination water.

Bob has his eyes peeled for any signs of card gambling. He is confident that he can make some serious money if he plays his cards right. He knows the key to success is to enter the gaming table unobtrusively, gain trust as a friendly sportsman, then go in for a series of kills. They won't know what hit them. He will need to get his good-natured friend to act as a decoy to start his hustle.

Bob tells Able. "It would be great fun to meet some of the guys and play a friendly poker game." Abel stops and thinks. Bob is an aggressive competitor when he plays poker. Bob likes to win. He is not the least bit friendly in a game of cards. Bob spies a group of men intent on playing a serious poker game. The cards are dealt quickly, and precisely, significant money is changing hands. No bullshit. Quiet is preferred. Bob tells Abel in a hushed tone. "I will spot you 50 dollars, try and stay in the game as long as you can." I figured out that he wanted to mule me into the game to size up the other players. I have got no problem with this, he can pay for my entertainment. At times, I can piss off serious card players by being too conservative in wagering bets. The first poker player to complain is our popular navy gunnery sergeant Warnisky. He looks me in the eye and then says. "You are slowing down our game, son." To the other players, he said. "How about we double the ante to 4 dollars and play no fast-fold." The 4 other players grunted in approval. So here it is: I didn't exactly know how to follow the rules. I looked over at Bob, hoping to quit. Instead, he just stood there grinning. So now I was committed to a poker game with many mean-talking card sharks. I didn't want to disappoint or waste Bob's generous gift of 50 dollars. That is much more money than I care to spend on a game of chance.

Regardless of a player's skill, luck can be with or against you. I had the good fortune of being really lucky on all accounts. Good cards kept coming my way. So when they didn't, I folded my cards as soon as the other players allowed me to. I then would glance over at Bob to see him studying the other players in deep concentration. It was as if he were burning images into his brain. After 2 hours of serious card playing, I had 140 dollars in cash in front of me. I had made 90 dollars profit on Bob's 50-dollar investment. I feigned a stomach flu. I told those card sharks. "You don't want me to puke on a table full of cash." Then I left and did my best to avoid those gamblers. I heard them all snickering as Bob took my place at the poker table. Bob thought to himself as he began to play poker. "Oh my, what a lucky day." I will get my 50 bucks back from Abel and have the table softened up for an evening of gambling." Bob was welcomed as a player. Predators know to look for prey. They had pushed out Abel with a minimum of expense. The foursome still had 98 potential applicants to profit amongst shipmates, and the ship had just left Port.

The next day the poker guys fully expected to see Bob Hansen back at the game table. He fits right in. Sergeant Warnisky was the first to speak to Bob. "My name at this table is 'Warrior'. The guys here decided to call you, 'Fuego.' "A little warning to others, hot fire. Bud Battles is 'Rhino' "He tells African safari stories. Last of all is Susan Quinn, she is one of the guys. You don't have to bite your tongue around her. She is our Galley Chief, tough as nails. We call her 'B.O.B' Bossy Old Bitch." Fuego sized her up. Middle age, short, cropped hair, a masculine jaw, and no sign of femininity. Fuego did not know that she was in the game by the recommendation of the Skipper Don Blanque. Earlier, the Skipper pulled Susan Quinn aside. He had a job for her. He asked. "Can I get you to trade places with Jon Johnsen at the guy's poker table?" Jon can watch the galley during your absence. "I need you to keep an eye on this new guy that they call Fuego." Don Blanque had absolute faith and conviction in Ms. Quinn's abilities to keep the card games friendly.

Today the card sharks plan to lay low and let the new guy settle in. Sergeant Warnisky suggested they split up and bring some fresh money from less-skilled poker players. Word travels fast on a ship. Novice players know who the card sharks are. They often shun serious players by playing separately with small coin wagers and out and out refuse to play predator poker. Instead, the card sharks find some small action that brings in a few dollars. This is different from what they are in the game for. They are looking for high-risk and significant gains. Tomorrow something interesting will come along.

That evening Susan Quinn was able to get away from the gaming table and bake a pork chop and stuffing dinner for the crew. She consistently receives a lot of compliments when meat is cooked fresh. Not from a can. The dish is tasty and served with a flour pork fat rue creamy gravy.

Susan Quinn let herself into the Captain's Quarters with a knock on the door and said. "Skipper, the sharks were calm as lambs today." Don Blanque replied. "I gathered that. I still want you to step in when the serious money is on the table. Can do."

Replied Susan. The Skipper had ship-shape work party plans for tomorrow, complete with inspections. No time for games.

It has been 10 days at Sea for the many merchant ships being escorted by the full armament power of a Navy escort. As they approach the southern passage of the Hawaiian Islands, there will be no stopping for R and R, Rest and Relaxation. No, each merchant marine ship has secreted cargo to advance the war front destined for separate Ports. In 10 days, they will be in the Marianas Islands. Don is confident his new ship and crew will see action. Some of them for the first time. May God help them.

Sergeant Warnisky put the word out during breakfast. Tonight's game is on. Serious players only are welcome at the poker game table. The Skipper has made sure that Quinn will be in the game. He coached her. "No funny stuff." This game is going to be a showdown between Warnisky and Hansen. The sharks are in the water. Beware.

Seated at the table is the gang of four. Sergeant Warnisky, 'Warrior'. To his right Bob Hansen, 'Fuego'. To his right, Bud Battles, 'Rhino,' and placed between Bud and the Sergeant sits Susan Quinn, known as 'B.O.B,' the Bossy Old Bitch.

There are no complaints about Warrior starting out as the dealer. He calls out the rules and quickly deals 5 cards to each player. "5 Dollars ante, no wild cards. Five-card draw. Initially, the group of 4 are conservative in betting. All winnings are kept on the table. This in an instance allows each player to gauge how they are doing. An hour into the game B.O.B and Rhino have the most money in front of them. Neither Warrior or Fuego seem the least bit worried. During the second hour of play Rhino decides it's time to share some of his safari adventures with the players. Rhino starts out saying. "Africa is the most magnificent place to experience for those inclined. You all really should go there someday. However, I doubt that is ever going to happen. So please allow me to share some of the highlights If I may.

This could be a turning point in this high-stakes poker game. Several of the crew join around the table to watch. Many of the crew of 102 are first-timers serving together on the American Kate's maiden voyage. This is free entertainment for the spectators. Rhino is sober, slick of the tongue, and aiming to please and distract. Rhino is holding 3 of a kind and hoping to take them to the bank. B.O.B thinks Rhino is up to fluster for a purpose. She has nothing sound in her card hand. She announces. "I'm sitting this one out." B.O.B thinks it is worth my 5-dollar ante to hear what Rhino says and not play.

Warrior looks at Rhino as if to say. "What the hell. I'm in." Rhino is the dealer, he announces. "The dealer takes no cards." Warrior says. "I'll take 2 cards."

Fuego asks for 3 cards. The other players figure he's got shit for cards. Perhaps Warrior has 3 of a kind. Nobody has a clue what Rhino has. Betting is fierce. Surprisingly Fuego is still in the game. Is he bluffing?

The players pause to hear Rhino speak. "Zanzibar, Africa is where you want to start your safari." Akama is my personal guide and dinner companion for each evening. I might add that dinner is served under canvas in the wildest places and served with the finest China and silver, including crystal-poured French wines and sumptuous brandies. You might be gored or devoured the next day by an African beast. If so, you want your last meal to be a formidable feast. The Zanzibar warrior travel guides provide the most outstanding protection against beast or man. They can converse freely with many other tribesmen. "I have 2 trophy heads displayed in my home. The Lion head and the Rhino head, which I am most proud of."

Rhino described the next day's hunt. "To the casual observer, the lion appears as the most formidable beast hanging on the wall. "The night before I killed my lion, I scarcely slept. The damn lions roared deafeningly loud throughout the night." "I told my guide, Akama, the next morning that I didn't sleep well and might not shoot as well as I should."

Akama said. "Not to worry, you go back to bed. We will take a large carcass to feed the lions then you can go shoot the lazy old lion. I returned to my bed. I Heard the sound of a rifle. I then slept in quiet solitude. I got up and went out to shoot my lion. Bang bang. Easy peasy. Later I will tell you about the dangers of Rhino hunting."

Fuego looked at his cards. He had shit to deal with. Fuego said. "Great story Rhino I fold. Good luck to you Rhino." Rhino and Warrior are ready to call and show their cards. Warrior displays three 6s. A smiling Rhino lays down three lucky 7s to win the hand. He still has the Rhino story in his repertoire.

The gang of four decides to take a short break. They have trust in themselves. Cash remains on the table as they use the facilities one by one. The players can eat or drink anything they want. They have all chosen not to drink. This is tournament poker with big money at stake. Clear heads prevail.

Warrior looks at his dwindling stash of cash. He needs to make some money soon or be done for the night. He pours himself a black coffee spiked generously with sugar. He is ready to focus on getting his money back when he returns. He can't help noticing that Fuego is sitting on a bigger pile of cash. It is his turn to call the game. Warrior calls 7 card draws. He will get two more cards to gamble with. After the low and high card bids, they discard down to 5 cards. There is a show of cards. Warrior proudly displays a full house of 3 kings and a pair of 7s. He is ready to take his winnings. B.O.B says. "My 4, 3 of a kind beats your full house." Betting was heavy. It takes an adjustment when the probability of a good hand goes up. Warrior groaned in dissatisfaction.

Fuego called 5 card draws. He thought I would keep it simple and hope to get lucky. He dealt a round of cards, then paused to look at his hand. He kept 2 Aces, then discarded 3 cards. Making it obvious he was only holding a matching pair at best. Warrior, Rhino, and B.O.B all ganged up on Fuego, the leader. Bud called out loudly. "I think it is time for my namesake story."

"We ate well on Safari because we had the best African hunters bringing back fresh, exotic meat. Meat so sumptuous and tender you would have to be there to know." Said Bud. "I already mentioned they served the best French wines and brandies. Nothing is finer than a glass of Portuguese Royal Oporto 14 years in the bottle. Good enough to be imported by Her Royal Majesty the Queen."

The following day, I was up bright and early. I was ready to go out and kill a Rhino. Akama had assembled armaments and the Zanzibar warriors. The Rover driver and his assistant located a Rhino for today's hunt very early in the morning. Provisions are already loaded. In 30 minutes, the search begins. When I first left the Rover, all I could see was a grey mass in the tall grass. I was told. Move quietly as to not startle the Rhino. It was all hush-hush and stealth as we saw the beast's immensity. In a whispered tone, I was handed the loaded rifle and told, 'Your aim must be good. The Bullet needs to enter past the collar bone and pierce the heart, ok?'

I said OK and took the shot. Then holy shit. The Rhino is headed straight at me. The damn Zanzibar army is running away to my right as fast as they can move. My faithful guide, Akama, threw me a loaded elephant gun and scampered off to my left. I was all alone, facing a killer Rhino that wanted me dead. I had to time my shot to drop him before he obliterated me." I aimed for his chest, squeezed the trigger, and blew a hole in him the size of my head. I kid you not, the beast collapsed so close to me I was splattered in blood. Then I did what every respectable hunter might do. I collapsed into exhaustion. When I awakened, I was in the Rover with a group of very drunken African Tribesmen. I

was quite the hero, voted for the best shot of the
year. Bud's Battles was overcome with emotion
after his narration. He received a standing ovation
and 3 hoorahs.

The group of four decided they could not top the
Rhino. So, it was time to gather the cards and call it
a night. Susan Quinn stopped by Skipper's cabin to
say good night. Don told her. "You did a good job
tonight." Also, he thought Bud's Rhino story was
told with posh dignity. " All in all, an excellent night.

Chapter 14

Guadalcanal

January 29, 1943

Loose lips sink ships. For security reasons, no one should ever give out the destination or disclose what cargo a vessel may carry. Doing so would endanger everyone aboard the ship and possibly compromise an entire mission. So, Captain Donald Blanque needed to exercise the utmost caution when he made the American Kate available to send armaments and supplies to Guadalcanal. Don's only son is serving on this hotly contested Island. So, who other than Donald Blanque could better ensure the safe transport of armaments and goods to this Outpost?

The Skipper's son, Lieutenant Norman Blanque, finds himself isolated and stuck in a hellhole with possibly the only way out is to be dead, wrapped in an American flag. It is one thing to engage the enemy. It is another thing to drive an embedded enemy that has been dug in and ready to fight since May 1942.

January 29th, the American Kate pulls anchor. She travels a short distance to unload her cargo for the final battle of taking Guadalcanal from the Japanese-held territory. August 7th, 1942, primarily United States Marines working with a small campaign of Allied troops landed to fight the enemy in the southern Solomon Islands. In May of 1942, a surprised Japanese Emperor launched a counteroffensive. Fighting was fierce. The battle was engaged by Navy Destroyers and Aircraft carriers at sea and on land, first by Marines, then later by the U.S. Army.

On January 29th, the Skipper Don Blanque, disguised as a humble longshoreman, grabs a cargo load and makes his way to the dock. After unloading his cargo, Don approaches Marine Sergeant Byron Haig and asks. "Can you help me get in touch with my son Marine Lieutenant Norman Blanque?" Byron responds. "I honestly don't give a rat's ass; we have got a war to fight." Don Blanque's blood began to boil. He spoke. "You will not address a senior officer in this fashion. I am the Captain and Commander of the American Kate!"

A newly humbled Byron Haig asked, "May I see the palms of your hands, sir?" Byron could plainly see these were not the hands of a dock worker.

Byron Haig snapped to attention, crisply saluted a ranking officer then asked. "How may I be of assistance, Sir?"

There is a good reason there is a chain of command. Priorities are made and then carried out efficiently. Such was the case for the Skipper getting the proper help to find and reunite with his son. However, rank does have its privileges.

Back aboard his ship Captain Blanque showered and shaved, then put on a freshly laundered dress white uniform to welcome his son aboard ship. He would see that his son would be treated to family leave. The first sight of his son demonstrated that he had enough of this war. His son is a proud serving U.S. Marine officer. We will need men like him to strengthen the economy moving forward.

The End

ACKNOWLEDGEMENTS

*I would like to dedicate this book to my parents,
Jack and Rosalie Kerr, who volunteered a decade
of service assisting the Bellingham S.S. Discovery
Sea Scout ship and who raised me with the love of
all boats that float.*

*Furthermore, I will always be in debt to the
outstanding service of Mr. & Mrs. Skipper Don
White of the S.S. Discovery Sea Scout Ship.
Bellingham, Washington. U.S.A.*

Thank you,

Able body seaman

Brian Kerr

Postscript

My father, Jack Kerr, loved his years in the Merchant Marine. He had the good fortune of shipping out with his best and closest friend, Bill Mack. These 2 sailors had the privilege of seeing much of the world traveling the Pacific and Atlantic oceans to ports far and near. In addition, they enjoyed the world's many ethnicities, including the Japanese post-war. I am struck by how fortunate they were to come home unscathed. Even when Dad told me of sighting a torpedo crossing the ship's bow. I asked. "Were you scared?" His reply was with a twinkle in his eye. NAHH.

My favorite of the many stories told by my dad is "The Black Bear" Dad passed away at the age of 93. So, I must do my best in the telling from earlier memories.

As a very young boy growing up in Seattle, Washington, I never grew tired of asking my dad to show his old black and white photographs of him and his childhood friend Bill Mack wrestling a black bear aboard a WWII Liberty ship.

Dad began the story.

First of all, Bill Mack and I joined the Merchant Marine service at 19 each. The United States Military fully commissioned the Marine Service as a separate division of the Armed Services. Bill and I wanted to serve our country and see the world. We shipped out both from the West and East coast traveling the Pacific and Atlantic Oceans far off to many distant lands. We served aboard many Liberty ships for 4 years, 1942-1946. Transporting foreign troops and calling on many ports, I learned of the universal good in humanity. I remember after the war ended, being in Tokyo, Japan. Our ship's crew was given a Japanese Judo Exhibition. They asked for volunteers to come up and experience a Karate lesson. I remember one crew member twice mocking and throwing punches. The Karate demonstrator threw the belligerent man on his ass. We all applauded.

The war is over. Please, let's move on. I watched a torpedo pass in front of our Liberty Ship. I cried out, Sub attack! Our Naval personnel dropped depth charges off of the stern. Later debris floated up. We circled, searching for survivors. I remember that day well. Years later, my wife Rosalie and I vacationed in Germany. We were Able to find records of that German submarine lost at that date and location, no survivors. My wife and I have German Ancestry. We could have had distant relatives aboard that submarine laid to rest at the bottom of the ocean.

We were so fortunate, and to think Bill and I were even fortunate to befriend a black bear. We saved that bear's life twice and were given a baby black bear. Perhaps from a closed zoo or an orphan in a hunting campaign? {I'm not sure.} Quickly, the bear became friends with the entire crew. Cute and cuddly at first. Then frolicking and tumbling, so we taught bear to wrestle. A handful of wrestlers participated at first. Later just Bill and I were up to the fight. The bear loved to win the battle and always did.

The Skipper called me into his cabin to talk. He said, Jack, that bear of yours is getting too damn big. Somebody could get hurt. The day will come when I expect you to find a new home for it.

Bill, the bear, and I did our best to hang low for a while. Unfortunately, the Galley Chief and I have a running feud.

One day, the Galley Chief came up the ladder from below deck carrying a fat sandwich stuffed with ham. The sandwich hoisted above him. The bear charged, then took the man's lunch with a mighty swipe of his great paw. No one was going to deny a treat from the bear.

Right then I knew what Bill and I had to do. Bear needed a new home. We convinced the Skipper to head to the Port of San Diego. Next stop for Bear, the San Diego Zoo. We are going to miss you bear.

Jack Stanford Kerr

Merchant Marine, First Class, Deck Officer

A New Start

Bob and Abel watched as the 1941 burgundy Plymouth coupe motored northward until it disappeared. Bob said. "Dad sure looked happy sitting next to his sweetheart."

Able replied. "Yeah, I don't expect they will be back anytime soon. It was marvellous while at home port to have such a fine set of wheels to sport about in. You have a great dad, Bob."

"Yes, I do," he replied. Then Bob added. "We kept the coupe looking like new and always on the ready for dad's return." Bob asked. "Do you want to come in for a beer?"

Abel responded to this question by walking into Bob's home, then reaching into the fridge for a cold brew. Enough was said for today concerning the loss of the Plymouth. Also left unsaid, what will they do with their lives now that they are resigned from the Merchant Marines?

Abel and Kate had a delicious cup of hot coffee to sip and enjoy. Far below, a bed of fog nestled in the San Francisco Bay. On their cottage hilltop, the sun was brilliant and seemed to greet robins tweeting a song and the chit-chittering of the white-crowned sparrow. It felt so good to do nothing but be in the moment.

Kate looked out over the pathway leading up to the cottage doorway. She said, "isn't that Bob walking to our home."

Abel replied, "yes, it is." Bob's shoulders are rounded into a slump. There is no sign of a parked car. Bob has never taken the bus here. There seems to be no taxi drop-off either. "I have never known Bob to travel in a bus, it is completely foreign to him."

Bob let himself into the cottage, then called out. "Good morning, Kate and Able." Bob fumbled around for a coffee cup, found a mug he liked, then poured a cup of morning joe. Abel pulled out a chair for his friend. Bob situated himself comfortably and then took a slurp of his coffee. After swallowing, he took a large breath and exhaled a mournful sigh. Bob said nothing. Bob always had something to say. Abel thought it best not to talk about his missing car or bus ride. So, Abel buoyantly announced. "How about those

Democrats?" Abel said this because Bob always is an enthused Democrat.

To Kate and Able's astonishment, Bob's response was, "There will never be another President Roosevelt, even Theodore Roosevelt , a Republican, was a great President."

Abel responded. "Certainly, there are many other Roosevelts, and a promising candidate can be found."

Bob replied. "All the remaining Roosevelt family members care about is making money. It's no good anymore." Abel thought about Mrs. Elanor Roosevelt. Abel thought it best to bite his tongue; he was sure Bob was not looking for that leadership. Instead, Abel decided to confront his friend outright.

"Bob, you are in a piss poor mood."

To which Bob replied, "Yes, I am." It appeared that even the birds quit their praise for the day and flew off for a more appreciative audience.

Abel thought the day was early. No sense in offering good booze to such a sour soul. Abel had seen his friend angry and sad before. This, however, felt different. Bob lingered for another cup of coffee. Bob eventually thought he needed to show some promise of a sunny disposition. Bob said at some point, "I need to purchase my own car."

Abel said. "I don't mean to pry, but don't you have a chunk of money left over from poker earnings and wages?"

Bob said. "Yes, I do, I'm just not ready to spend it."

Able replied. "I think it is time you bought a new set of wheels, Bob." Later when Bob returned to his cheerful self, Abel made a request. "Bob, I am hopeful you can teach me how to operate a clutch and shift transmission when you find your new car. Bob left the Shellhorn cottage with a slightly elevated mood. Tomorrow is a new day.

The very next day, Bob awoke early and hopped out of bed. The first thing he did was to put in a telephone call to his dad in Seattle, WA. "Good morning, Dad. I just wanted you to know that I hope to buy my first new car today. My good friend Abel and I certainly appreciated driving your new Plymouth Coupe. You kind of spoiled me, Dad. I just don't want to go out and buy some piece of junk. I have been saving money from the Great War Years; I have a little over $1000 to spend on a new car."

Bob heard his dad chuckle over the phone, then say. "How much money do you need, son?"

"I have my eyes set on a Mercury convertible priced at $1495."

Dad replied, "That sounds reasonable enough, son. I suggest you hammer out the deal that will work for you, and I will transfer the balance needed to you." After hanging up the phone, Bob's dad thought owning his first new car should be memorable. He was glad he could afford to help his son and knew that Bob would take good care of his investment. When he left for Boeing Aerospace, a generous smile joined him on his drive to work.

A taxicab pulled up to take Bob to Van Etta Motors on 1101 Van Ness Avenue. February 1, 1946, 8:55 AM. 5 minutes before opening, Bob gave the driver a respectable tip and destination fee, then marched to the showroom. There before Bob's eyes, parked on a pedestal, stood the 1946 Mercury convertible. It had just arrived here in the San Francisco showroom. Bob Hansen and the sales representative were the only two people there. The salesman wore a black shirt and a shiny black belt on his top half tucked into a pair of white pants and polished white patent leather shoes below his belt. His outfit was complemented by a sizable gold watch and a matching gold name tag. The name tag suggested he is named Damien. Damien asked Bob. "Are you here to buy a car?"

Bob responded bluntly. "Yes, this one." Bob pointed directly at the yellow chiffon convertible, the only car in the showroom.

Damien responded with an audible hiss noise, then said. "It might not be for sale."

Bob, now ill-humored, responded. "Clearly, the price is listed as $1495." The price tag stood in the window, written in large enough letters to be seen from across the street. Bob said, "I am prepared to pay the full cash price for this car today." Now more than ever, Bob became combative and then said. "Why not today?"

Again, Damien clearly hissed at him and then replied. "With only 6,044 Mercury convertibles available worldwide, we need time to show the car to lure customers such as yourself into showing off our entire line of luxury cars. This car really is splendid."

Bob had quite enough of this. He did an about-face, then found Mr. Van Etta or whoever was in charge. The sign on the door read Manager of Sales. Bob knocked and then quickly entered the sales office. Bob needed a fresh start. He said with his warmest smile. "Good morning, I'm Bob Hansen. I am here to pave over a few details so we can come to an understanding concerning the promotion and sale of your showroom Mercury. I have been made aware that you need a limited amount of display time to recoup your investment in bringing the car to display. Here are my terms. Today I will pay $1495 plus taxes and license fees for the showroom Mercury. You can show the car as sold with no additional miles added for the next 30 days. On the first of March, I will drive away in my new car."

The Sales Manager, Mr. Van Zandt, thoughtfully scratched his chin, thinking. "Damien is not going to like this, but I think the terms are reasonable." Both men stood up. Mr. Van Zandt said. "We have ourselves a deal." The contracts and paperwork were signed. Bob left after shaking hands to cement the transaction. He was all too glad to avoid Damien on his way out.

On the first of March, Bob again arrived by taxi. Today he gets the keys. As agreed, no new miles are added to the Mercury convertible. Bob watches as his new car rolls off the pedestal and backs into the dealership parking lot. Mr. Van Zandt leaves his office to greet Bob. He said, "Damien left to work at the Cadillac Dealership. I know that you two did not get along well." Bob bit down on his tongue and listened. "I sure do hope you recommend us well and want to return for your next car here. Bob smiled in agreement, then took off with the V-8 100 hp rumbling. The mercury top was down, and Bob nestled into the leather seat with bright chrome trim surrounding the car glistening in the California sun. Passers-by took notice of the new vehicle. Some people waved to the man in his new car. Bob felt like a millionaire riding in a parade. It was glorious.

Abel announced to the world Carpe Diem. During Able's freshmen year at Cambridge College, first-year Latin students were expected to already know Carpe Diem, which means Seize the Day, and that was precisely what his intentions were. Able's primordial roots are already kicking in. Abel Shellhorn must go out today and realize his potential. The first thing to do is to sit down and enjoy the fruit of the gods, coffee. Kate joins him, then puts the kettle on for a fine cup of British tea. Kate completes her continental breakfast preparing a buttered English muffin topped with a teaspoon of marmalade. Abel toasts two generous slices of rye bread, then slathers them with butter. The late warm Spring California sunshine has already chased the fog from the San Francisco Bay, and it is not yet 7:00 AM.

Married for several years now, they often know the gist of what each will say next. Abel slurped his coffee, and Kate sipped her hot tea. Kate begins the morning conversation. "I want a piece of the action. I have signed up for a professional course on the Principles of Accounting."

Abel interjected. "That's great."

Kate continues speaking. "I have done well managing our household finances."

Abel replied. "Yes, you have."

Kate said. "I am confident I am the most trusted and best-qualified person to keep our money in the family. Now that men able to weld are back from the war, I find that the Kaiser Ship Builders have little need of me. I just don't see myself staying home out here in the boonies. Beaty next door cares so well for our son Allen. It is my hope you will let me in to carry the burden of the business finances."

Now it was Abel's turn to speak and have Kate's attention. "To be perfectly frank with you Kate, I couldn't be more relieved and thankful. I have spent literally hours thinking about expanding our shipping business. I too need to shift my labor from being aboard ships to managing a business that can grow. You can count on my full support going forward. As soon as you like you can set up in our office space. All we really need is to add another chair.”

Kate saw her chance to jump into Abel’s conversation. When Abel got to thinking and talking, he wasn’t always the best listener. She said, “Today is Sunday. It is a fine day for us to putter in the office. You can show me how things are organised. Then on Monday, I can attend my Accounting Principles class. You can go forth as an invigorated Shellhorn Shipping Executive. I would like to offer you Beaty and our son Allen your favorite dinner, Beef pot roast with carrots and gravied new potatoes.”

Abel responded. “Oh Goody! I have the perfect wine to serve, a 6-year-aged Napa Valley Cabernet Sauvignon.” Kate rushed off to preheat the oven and then slow-cook the pot roast.

While Kate and Abel puttered in the office, Abel requested from Kate. “Would it be ok to bring on Bob Hansen as a full partner to Shellhorn Shipping? I would like to offer Bob a modest salary and profit sharing.

Kate replied. “Bob Hansen and you are like a couple of brothers. Of course, it is ok.”